To Love and Be Wise

Josephine Tey is one of the best known and best loved of all crime writers. She began to write full-time after the successful publication of her first novel, *The Man in the Queue* (1929), which introduced Inspector Grant of Scotland Yard. In 1937 she returned to crime writing with *A Shilling for Candles*, but it wasn't until after the Second World War that the majority of her crime novels were published. Josephine Tey died in 1952, leaving her entire estate to the National Trust.

Praise for Josephine Tey

'A detective story with a very considerable difference. Ingenious, stimulating and very enjoyable' *Sunday Times*

'One of the best mysteries of all time' *New York Times*

'As interesting and enjoyable a book as they will meet in a month of Sundays' *Observer*

'First-rate mystery, ably plotted and beautifully written' *Los Angeles Times*

'Suspense is achieved by unexpected twists and extremely competent storytelling . . . credible and convincing' *Spectator*

'Really first class . . . a continual delight' *Times Literary Supplement*

'Josephine Tey enjoys a category to herself, as a virtuoso in the spurious . . . the nature of the deception on this occasion is too good to give away' *New Statesman*

'Tey's style and her knack for creating bizarre characters are

JOSEPHINE TEY

To Love and Be Wise

arrow books

Published by Arrow Books 2011

1 3 5 7 9 10 8 6 4 2

First published in Great Britain in 1950 by
Peter Davies Ltd

Arrow Books
Random House, 20 Vauxhall Bridge Road
London SW1V 2SA

www.randomhouse.co.uk

Addresses for companies within The Random House Group Limited can be found at:
www.randomhouse.co.uk/offices.htm

The Random House Group Limited Reg. No. 954009

A CIP catalogue record for this book
is available from the British Library

ISBN 9780099556749

The Random House Group Limited supports The Forest Stewardship
Council (FSC®), the leading international forest certification organisation.
Our books carrying the FSC label are printed on FSC® certified paper.
FSC is the only forest certification scheme endorsed by the leading
environmental organisations, including Greenpeace. Our
paper procurement policy can be found at
www.randomhouse.co.uk/environment

MIX
Paper from
responsible sources
FSC® C016897

Printed and bound in Great Britain by Clays Ltd, St Ives PLC

I

GRANT paused with his foot on the lowest step, and listened to the shrieking from the floor above. As well as the shrieks there was a dull continuous roar; an elemental sound, like a forest fire or a river in spate. As his reluctant legs bore him upwards he arrived at the inevitable deduction: the party was being a success.

He was not going to the party. Literary sherry parties, even distinguished ones, were not Grant's cup of tea. He was going to collect Marta Hallard and take her out to dinner. Policemen, it is true, do not normally take out to dinner leading actresses who gravitate between the Haymarket and the Old Vic; not even when the police-men are Detective-Inspectors at Scotland Yard. There were three reasons for his privileged position, and Grant was aware of all three. In the first place he was a present-able escort, in the second place he could afford to dine at Laurent's, and in the third place Marta Hallard did not find it easy to obtain escort. For all her standing, and her chic, men were a little afraid of Marta. So when Grant, a mere Detective-Sergeant then, appeared in her life over a matter of stolen jewellery, she had seen to it that he did not entirely fade out of it again. And Grant had been glad to stay. If he was useful to Marta as a cavalier when she needed one, she was even more useful to him as a window on the world. The more windows on the world a policeman has the better he is likely to be at his job, and Marta was Grant's 'leper's squint' on the theatre.

The roar of the party's success came flooding out through the open doors on to the landing, and Grant paused to look at the yelling crowd asparagus-packed into the long Georgian room and to wonder how he was going to pry Marta out of it.

Just inside the door, baffled apparently by the solid wall of talking and drinking humanity, was a young man, looking lost. He still had his hat in his hand, and had therefore just arrived.

'In difficulties?' Grant said, catching his eye.

'I've forgotten my megaphone,' the young man said.

He said it in a gentle drawl, not bothering to compete with the crowd. The mere difference in pitch made the words more audible than if he had shouted. Grant glanced at him again, approvingly. He was a very good-looking young man indeed, now that he took notice. Too blond to be entirely English. Norwegian, perhaps?

Or American. There was something in the way he said 'forgotten' that was transatlantic.

The early spring afternoon was already blue against the windows and the lamps were lit. Across the haze of cigarette smoke Grant could see Marta at the far end of the room listening to Tullis the playwright telling her about his royalties. He did not have to hear what Tullis was talking about to know that he was talking about his royalties; that is all Tullis ever talked about. Tullis could tell you, off-hand, what the Number Two company of his *Supper for Three* took on Easter Monday in Blackpool in 1938. Marta had given up even a pretence of listening,

6

and her mouth drooped at the corners. Grant thought that if that D.B.E. did not come along soon Marta would be disappointed into the need for a face-lifting. He decided to stay where he was until he could catch her eye. They were both tall enough to see over the heads of a normal crowd.

With a policeman's ingrained habit of inspection he let his eye run over the crowd between them, but found nothing of interest. It was the usual collection. The very prosperous firm of Ross and Cromarty were celebrating the publication of Lavinia Fitch's twenty-first book, and since it was largely due to Lavinia that the firm was prosperous the drinks were plentiful and the guests were distinguished. Distinguished in the sense of being well-dressed and well-known, that is to say. The distinguished in achievement did not celebrate the birth of *Maureen's Lover*, nor drink the sherry of Messrs Ross and Cromarty. Even Marta, that inevitable Dame, was here because she was a neighbour of Lavinia's in the country. And Marta, bless her black-and-white chic and her disgruntled look, was the nearest thing to real distinction in the room.

Unless, of course, this young man whom he did not know brought more than good looks to the party. He wondered what the stranger did for a living. An actor? But an actor would not stand baffled at the edge of a crowd. And there was something in the implied comment of his remark about the megaphone, in the detachment with which he was watching the scene, that divorced him from his surroundings. Was it possible, Grant wondered, that those cheekbones were being wasted in a stockbroker's office? Or was it perhaps that the soft

7

light of Messrs Ross and Cromarty's expensive lamps flattered that nice straight nose and the straight blond hair and that the young man was less beautiful in the daylight?

'Perhaps you can tell me,' said the young man, still not raising his voice in emulation, 'which is Miss Lavinia Fitch?'

Lavinia was the sandy little woman by the middle window. She had bought herself a fashionable hat for the occasion, but had done nothing to accommodate it; so that the hat perched on her bird's-nest of ginger hair as if it had dropped there from an upper window as she walked along the street. She was wearing her normal expression of pleased bewilderment and no make-up.

Grant pointed her out to the young man.

'Stranger in town?' he said, borrowing a phrase from all good Westerns. The polite formality of 'Miss Lavinia Fitch' could have come only from the U.S.A.

'I'm really looking for Miss Fitch's nephew. I looked him up in the book and he isn't there, but I hoped he'd be here. Do you happen to know him, Mr ——?'

'Grant.'

'Mr Grant?'

'I know him by sight, but he isn't here. Walter Whitmore, you mean?'

'Yes. Whitmore. I don't know him at all, but I want very much to meet him because we have—had, I mean—a great friend in common. I was sure he'd be here. You're quite sure he isn't? After all, it's quite a party.'

'He isn't in this room; I know that, because Whitmore is as tall as I am. But he may still be around somewhere. Look, you had better come and meet Miss Fitch. I suppose we can get through the barricade if we have the determination.'

'You lean and I'll squirm,' said the young man, referring to their respective build. 'This is very kind of you, Mr Grant,' he said as they came up for air half-way, wedged tightly together between the hedged elbows and shoulders of their fellows; and he laughed up at the helpless Grant. And Grant was suddenly disconcerted. So disconcerted that he turned immediately and continued his struggle through the jungle to the clearing at the middle window where Lavinia Fitch was standing.

'Miss Fitch,' he said, 'here is a young man who wants to meet you. He is trying to get in touch with your nephew.'

'With Walter?' said Lavinia, her peaked little face losing its muzzy expression of general benevolence and sharpening to real interest.

'My name is Searle, Miss Fitch. I'm over from the States on holiday and I wanted to meet Walter because Cooney Wiggin was a friend of mine too.'

'Cooney! You are a friend of Cooney's? Oh, Walter will be delighted, my dear, simply delighted. Oh, what a nice surprise in the middle of this—I mean, so unexpected. Walter *will* be pleased. Searle, did you say?'

'Yes. Leslie Searle. I couldn't find Walter in the book——'

'No, he has just a pied-à-terre in town. He lives down at Salcott St Mary like the rest of us. Where he has the farm, you know. The farm he broadcasts about. At least it's my farm but he runs it and talks about it and——. He's broadcasting this afternoon, that is why he isn't

9

coming to the party. But you must come down and stay. Come down this weekend. Come back with us this afternoon.'

'But you don't know if Walter——'

'You don't have any engagements for the weekend, do you?'

'No. No, I haven't. But——'

'Well, then. Walter is going straight back from the studio, but you can come with Liz and me in our car and we'll surprise him. Liz! Liz, dear, where are you? Where are you staying, Mr Searle?'

'I'm at the Westmorland.'

'Well, what could be handier. Liz! Where *is* Liz?'

'Here, Aunt Lavinia.'

'Liz, dear, this is Leslie Searle, who is coming back with us for the weekend. He wants to meet Walter because they were both friends of Cooney's. And this is Friday, and we are all going to be at Salcott over the weekend recovering from this—being nice and quiet and peaceful, so what could be more appropriate. So, Liz dear, you take him round to the Westmorland and help him pack and then come back for me, will you? By that time this—the party will surely be over, and you can pick me up and we'll go back to Salcott together and surprise Walter.'

Grant saw the interest in the young man's face as he looked at Liz Garrowby, and wondered a little. Liz was a small plain girl with a sallow face. True, she had remarkable eyes; speedwell blue and surprising; and she had the kind of face a man might want to live with; she was a nice girl, Liz. But she was not the type of girl at whom young men look with instant attention. Perhaps it was just that Searle had heard rumours of her engagement, and was identifying her as Walter Whitmore's fiancée.

He lost interest in the Fitch ménage as he saw that Marta had spotted him. He indicated that he would meet her at the door, and plunged once more into the suffocating depths. Marta, being the more ruthless of the two, did the double distance in half the time and was waiting for him in the doorway.

'Who is the beautiful young man?' she asked, looking backwards as they moved to the stairs.

'He came looking for Walter Whitmore. He says he's a friend of Cooney Wiggin.'

'*Says?*' repeated Marta, being caustic not about the young man but about Grant.

'The police mind,' Grant said apologetically.

'And who is Cooney Wiggin, anyhow?'

'Cooney was one of the best-known press photographers in the States. He was killed while photographing one of those Balkan flare-ups a year or two ago.'

'You know everything, don't you.'

It was on the tip of Grant's tongue to say: 'Anyone but an actress would have known that,' but he liked Marta. Instead he said: 'He is going down to Salcott for the weekend, I understand.'

'The beautiful young man? Well, well. I hope Lavinia knows what she is doing.'

'What is wrong with having him down?'

'I don't know, but it seems to me to be taking risks with their luck.'

'Luck?'

'Everything has worked out the way they wanted it to,

hasn't it? Walter saved from Marguerite Merriam and settling down to marry Liz; all family together in the old homestead and too cosy for words. No time to go introducing disconcertingly beautiful young men into the ménage, it seems to me.'

'Disconcerting,' murmured Grant, wondering again what had disconcerted him about Searle. Mere good looks could not have been responsible. Policemen are not impressed by good looks.

'I wager that Emma takes one look at him and gets him out of the house directly after breakfast on Monday morning,' Marta said. 'Her darling Liz is going to marry Walter, and nothing is going to stop that if Emma has anything to do with it.'

'Liz Garrowby doesn't look very impressionable to me. I don't see why Mrs Garrowby should worry.'

'Don't you indeed. That boy was making an impression on me in thirty seconds flat and a range of twenty yards, and I'm considered practically incombustible. Besides, I never believed that Liz really fell in love with that stick. She just wanted to bind up his broken heart.'

'Was it badly broken?'

'Considerably shaken, I should say. Naturally.'

'Did you ever act with Marguerite Merriam?'

'Oh, yes. More than once. We were together for quite a lengthy run in *Walk in Darkness*. There's a taxi coming.'

'*Taxi!* What did you think of her?'

'Marguerite? Oh, she was mad, of course '

'How mad?'

'Ten tenths.'

'In what way?'

'You mean how did it take her? Oh, a complete indifference to everything but the thing she wanted at the moment.'

'That isn't madness; that is merely the criminal mind at its simplest.'

'Well, you ought to know, my dear. Perhaps she was a criminal manqué. What is quite certain is that she was as mad as a hatter and I wouldn't wish even Walter Whitmore a fate like being married to her.'

'Why do you dislike the British Public's bright boy so much?'

'My dear, I hate the way he *yearns*. It was bad enough when he was yearning over the thyme on an Aegean hillside with the bullets zipping past his ears—he never failed to let us hear the bullets: I always suspected that he did it by cracking a whip——'

'Marta, you shock me.'

'I don't, my dear; not one little bit. You know as well as I do. When we were *all* being shot at, Walter took care that he was safe in a nice fuggy office fifty feet underground. Then when it was once more unique to be in danger, up comes Walter from his little safe office and sits himself on a thymey hillside with a microphone and a whip to make bullet noises with.'

'I see that I shall have to bail you out, one of these days.'

'Homicide?'

'No; criminal libel.'

'Do you need bail for that? I thought it was one of those nice gentlemanly things that you are just summonsed for.'

Grant thought how independable Marta's ignorances were.

'It might still be homicide, though,' Marta said, in the cooing, considering voice that was her trade-mark on the stage. 'I could just stand the thyme and the bullets, but now that he has taken a ninety-nine years' lease of the spring corn, and the woodpeckers, and things, he amounts to a public menace.'

'Why do you listen to him?'

'Well, there's a dreadful fascination about it, you know. One thinks: Well, that's the absolute sky-limit of awfulness, than which *nothing* could be worse. And so next week you listen to see if it really *can* be worse. It's a snare. It's so awful that you can't even switch off. You wait fascinated for the next piece of awfulness, and the next. And you are still there when he signs off.'

'It couldn't be, could it, Marta, that this is mere professional jealousy?'

'Are you suggesting that the creature is a *professional*?' asked Marta, dropping her voice a perfect fifth, so that it quivered with the reflection of repertory years, and provincial digs, and Sunday trains, and dreary auditions in cold dark theatres.

'No, I'm suggesting that he is an actor. A quite natural and unconscious actor, who has made himself a household word in a few years without doing any noticeable work to that end. I could forgive you for not liking that. What did Marguerite find so wonderful about him?'

'I can tell you that. His devotion. Marguerite liked picking the wings off flies. Walter would let her take him to pieces and then come back for more.'

'There was one time that he didn't come back.'

14

'Yes.'

'What was the final row about, do you know?'

'I don't think there was one. I think he just told her he was through. At least that is what he said at the inquest. Did you read the obituaries, by the way?'

'I suppose I must have at the time. I don't remember them individually.'

'If she had lived another ten years she would have got a tiny par in among the "ads" on the back page. As it was she got better notices than Duse. "A flame of genius has gone out and the world is the poorer." "She had the lightness of a blown leaf and the grace of a willow in the wind." That sort of thing. One was surprised that there were no black edges in the Press. The mourning was practically of national dimensions.'

'It's a far cry from that to Liz Garrowby.'

'Dear, nice Liz. If Marguerite Merriam was too bad even for Walter Whitmore, then Liz is too good for him. Much too good for him. I should be delighted if the beautiful young man took her from under his nose.'

'Somehow I can't see your "beautiful young man" in the rôle of husband, whereas Walter will make a very good one.'

'My good man, Walter will broadcast about it. All about their children, and the shelves he has put up in the pantry, and how the little woman's bulbs are coming along, and the frost patterns on the nursery window. She'd be much safer with—what did you say his name was?'

'Searle. Leslie Searle.' Absentmindedly he watched the pale yellow neon signature of *Laurent*'s coming nearer.

'I don't think safe is the adjective I would apply to Searle, somehow,' he said reflectively; and from that moment forgot all about Leslie Searle until the day when he was sent down to Salcott St Mary to search for the young man's body.

2

'DAYLIGHT!' said Liz, coming out on to the pavement. 'Good clean daylight.' She sniffed the afternoon air with pleasure. 'The car is round the corner in the square. Do you know London well, Mr—Mr Searle?'

'I've been in England for holidays quite often, yes. Not often as early in the year as this, though.'

'You haven't seen England at all unless you have seen it in the spring.'

'So I've heard.'

'Did you fly over?'

'Just from Paris, like a good American. Paris is fine in the spring too.'

'So I've heard,' she said, returning his phrase and his tone. And then, finding the eye he turned on her intimidating, went on: 'Are you a journalist? Is that how you knew Cooney Wiggin?'

'No, I'm in the same line as Cooney was.'

'Press photography?'

'Not Press. Just photography. I spend most of the winter on the Coast, doing people.'

'The Coast?'

'California. That keeps me on good terms with my bank manager. And the other half of the year I travel and photograph the things I want to photograph.'

'It sounds a good sort of life,' Liz said, as she unlocked the car door and got in.

'It's a very good life.'

The car was a two-seater Rolls; a little old-fashioned in shape as Rolls cars, which last for ever, are apt to be. Liz explained it as they drove out of the square into the stream of the late afternoon traffic.

'The first thing Aunt Lavinia did when she made money was to buy herself a sable scarf. She had always thought a sable scarf the last word in good dressing. And the second thing she wanted was a Rolls. She got that with her next book. She never wore the scarf at all because she said it was a dreadful nuisance to have something dangling about her all the time, but the Rolls was a great success so we still have it.'

'What happened to the sable scarf?'

'She swopped it for a pair of Queen Anne chairs and a lawn-mower.'

As they came to rest in front of the hotel she said: 'They won't let me wait here. I'll go over to the parking place and wait for you.'

'But aren't you going to pack for me?'

'Pack for you? Certainly not.'

'But your aunt said you were to.'

'That was a mere figure of speech.'

'Not the way I figure it. Anyhow, come up and watch while I pack. Lend me your advice and countenance. It's a nice countenance.'

In the end it was actually Liz who packed the things into his two cases, while he took them out of the drawers and tossed them over to her. They were all very expensive things, she observed; custom-made of the best materials.

'Are you very rich, or just very extravagant?' she asked.

'Fastidious, let us say.'

By the time they left the hotel the first street lamps were decorating the daylight.

'This is when I think lights look best,' Liz said. 'While it is still daylight. They are daffodil yellow and magic. Presently when it grows dark they will go white and ordinary.'

They drove back to Bloomsbury only to find that Miss Fitch had gone. The Ross part of the firm, sprawled in large exhaustion in a chair and thoughtfully consuming what was left of the sherry, roused himself to a shadow of his professional bonhomie to say that Miss Fitch had decided that there would be more room in Mr Whitmore's car and had gone over to the studio to pick him up when he had finished his half-hour. Miss Garrowby and Mr Searle were to follow them down to Salcott St Mary.

Searle was silent as they made their way out of London; from deference to the driver, Liz supposed, and liked him for it. It was not until green fields appeared on either hand that he began to talk about Walter. Cooney, it seemed, had thought a lot of Walter.

'You weren't in the Balkans with Cooney Wiggin, then?'

'No, I knew Cooney back in the States. But he wrote me a lot in letters about your cousin.'

'That was nice of him. But Walter isn't my cousin, you know.'

'Not? But Miss Fitch is your aunt, isn't she?'

'No. I'm no relation to any of them. Lavinia's sister —Emma—married my father when I was little. That's all. Mother—Emma, that is—practically surrounded him, if the truth must be told. He didn't have a chance. You see, she brought up Lavinia, and it was a frightful shock to her when Vinnie upped and did something on her own. Especially anything so outré as becoming a best-seller. Emma looked round to see what else she could lay hands on that would do to go broody about, and there was Father, stranded with a baby daughter, and simply asking to be arrested. So she became Emma Garrowby, and my mother. I never think of her as my "step", because I don't remember any other. When my father died, mother came to live at Trimmings with Aunt Lavinia, and when I left school I took over the job of her secretary. Hence the line about packing for you.'

'And Walter? Where does he come in?'

'He is the eldest sister's son. His parents died in India and Aunt Lavinia has brought him up since then. I mean, since he was fifteen, or so.'

He was silent for a little, evidently disentangling this in his mind.

Why had she told him that, she wondered? Why had she told him that her mother was possessive; even if she had made it clear that she was possessive in the very nicest way? Was it possible that she was nervous? She, who was never nervous and never chattered. What was there to be nervous about? There was surely nothing disconcerting in the presence of a good-looking young man. Both as Liz Garrowby and as Miss Lavinia Fitch's secretary she had entertained a great many good-looking young men in her time, and had not been (as far as she could remember) greatly impressed.

She turned from the black polished surface of the

arterial road into a side one. The last raw scar of new development had faded behind them, and they were now in an altogether country world. The little lanes ran in and out of each other, anonymous and irrelevant, and Liz picked the ones she wanted without hesitation.

'How do you choose?' Searle asked. 'All these little dirt roads look alike to me.'

'They look alike to me too. But I have done this trip so often that my hands do it for me, the way my fingers know the keys of a typewriter. I couldn't repeat the keys of a typewriter by trying to visualise them, but my fingers know where each key is. Do you know this part of the world?'

'No, this is new to me.'

'It's a dull county, I think. Quite featureless. Walter says that it is a constant permutation of the same seven "props": six trees and a haystack. Indeed he says that there is a phrase in the county regiment's official march that says quite plainly: Six trees and a *hay*-stack!' She sang the phrase for him. 'But where you see the bump in the road is the beginning of Orfordshire, and that is much more satisfying.'

Orfordshire was in truth a satisfactory stretch of territory. In the growing dusk its lines flowed together in ever-changing combinations that were dream-like in their perfection. Presently they paused on the lip of a shallow valley and looked down on the dark smudge of roofs and the scattered lights of a village.

'Salcott St Mary,' Liz said, introducing it. 'A once beautiful English village that is now occupied territory.'

'Occupied by whom?'

'By what the remaining natives call "they artist folk".'

21

It is very sad for them, poor things. They took Aunt Lavinia in their stride, because she was the owner of the "big house" and not part of their actual lives at all. And she has been here so long that she is almost beginning to belong. The big house has never been part of the village in the last hundred years, anyhow, so it didn't matter much who lived in it. The rot started when the mill house fell vacant, and some firm was going to buy it for a factory. I mean: to turn it into a factory. Then Marta Hallard heard about it and bought it to live in, right under the various lawyers' noses, and everyone was delighted and thought they were saved. They didn't much want an actress creature living in the mill house, but at least they weren't after all to have a factory in their nice village. Poor darlings, if they could only have foreseen.'

She set the car in motion, and drove slowly along the slope, parallel with the village.

'I take it there was a sheep-track from London to here in about six months,' Searle said.

'How did you know?'

'I see it all the time on the Coast. Someone finds a good quiet spot, and before they've got the plumbing fixed they're being asked to vote for mayor.'

'Yes. Every third cottage in the place has an alien in it. All degrees of wealth, from Toby Tullis—the playwright, you know—who has a lovely Jacobean house in the middle of the village street, to Serge Ratoff the dancer who lives in a converted stable. All degrees of living in sin, from Deenie Paddington who never has the same weekend guest twice, to poor old Atlanta Hope and Bart Hobart who have been living in sin, bless them, for

the best part of thirty years. All degrees of talent from
Silas Weekley, who writes those dark novels of country
life, all steaming manure and slashing rain, to Miss
Easton-Dixon who writes a fairy-tale book once a year
for the Christmas trade.'

'It sounds lovely,' Searle said.

'It's obscene,' Liz said, more hotly than she intended;
and then wondered again why she should be so on edge
this evening. 'And talking of the obscene,' she said,
pulling herself together, 'I'm afraid it is too dark for you
to appreciate Trimmings, but the full flavour of it can
keep till the morning. You can just get the general
effect against the sky.'

She waited while the young man took in the frieze of
dark pinnacles and crenellations against the evening
sky. 'The special gem is the Gothic conservatory, which
you can't see in this light.'

'Why did Miss Fitch choose this?' Searle asked in wonder.

'Because she thought it was grand,' Liz said, her voice
warm with affection. 'She was brought up in a rectory,
you know; the kind of rectory that was built circa 1850;
so her eye became conditioned to Victorian Gothic.
Even now, you know, she doesn't honestly see what is
wrong with it. She knows people laugh at it, and she is
quite philosophical about it, but she doesn't really know
why they laugh. When she first brought Cormac Ross,
her publisher, here, he complimented her on the appro-
priateness of the name, and she had no idea what he was
talking about.'

'Well, I'm in no mood to be critical, even of Victorian
Gothic,' the young man said. 'It was extraordinarily nice
of Miss Fitch to have me down here without even stopping

23

to look me up in the reference books. Somehow over in the States we expect more caution from the English.'

'It isn't a matter of caution with the English; it's a matter of domestic calculation. Aunt Lavinia asked you down on the spur of the moment because she didn't have to do any domestic reckoning. She knows that there is enough spare linen to furnish a spare bed, and enough food in the house to feed a guest, and enough "labour" to provide for his comfort, and so she has no need to hesitate. Do you mind if we go straight round to the garage and take your things in through the side door. It's a day's march to the front door from the domestics' quarters, the baronial hall unfortunately intervening.'

'Who built this and why?' Searle asked, looking up at the bulk of the house as they skirted it.

'A man from Bradford, I understand. There was a very pleasant early Georgian house on the spot—there is a print of it in the gun-room—but he thought it a poor-looking object and pulled it down.'

So it was through ugly passages, dimly lit, that Searle carried his luggage; passages that Liz said always reminded her of boarding-school.

'Just drop them there,' she said, indicating a service stair, 'and someone will take them up presently. Come through now to comparative civilisation and get warm and have a drink and meet Walter.'

She pushed open a baize door and led him into the front of the house.

'Do you roller-skate?' he asked, as they crossed the meaningless spaces of the hall.

Liz said that she hadn't thought of it, but that the place was, of course, useful for dances. 'The local hunt use it once a year,' she said. 'Though you mightn't think it, it's less draughty than the Corn Exchange in Wickham.'

She opened a door and they went from the grey spaces of Orfordshire and the dreary dim corridors of the house into warmth and firelight and the welcome of a lived-in room full of well-used furniture and scented with burning logs and narcissi. Lavinia was sunk in a chair with her neat little feet on the edge of the steel fender and her untidy mop of hair escaping from its pins all over the cushions. Facing her, with his elbow on the mantelpiece and one foot on the fender in his favourite attitude, was Walter Whitmore, and Liz saw him with a rush of affection and relief.

Why relief? she asked herself, as she listened to the greetings. She had known Walter would be here. Why relief?

Was it just that she could now hand over the social burden to Walter?

But social duties were her daily task and she took them in her stride. Nor could Searle be justly considered a burden. She had rarely met anyone so easy or so undemanding. Why this gladness to see Walter, this absurd feeling that now it would be all right? Like a child coming back from strangeness to a familiar room.

She watched the pleasure on Walter's face as he welcomed Searle; and loved him. He was human, and imperfect, and his face was already growing lined, and his hair showed signs of growing back above the temples, but he was Walter, and real; not—not something of inhuman beauty that had walked out of some morning of the world beyond our remembering.

She took pleasure in remarking that, face to face with

25

Walter's tallness, the newcomer looked nearly short. And his shoes, for all their expensiveness were, from an English point of view, distinctly regrettable.

'After all, he's only a photographer,' she said to herself, and was caught up by her own absurdity.

Was she so impressed by Leslie Searle that she needed protection against him? Surely not.

It was not uncommon to find that morning-of-the-world beauty among northern peoples; nor was it to be wondered at that it made one think of tales of the seal people and their strangeness. The young man was just a good-looking Scandinavian-American with a deplorable taste in shoes and a talent for using the right kind of lens. There was not the slightest need for her to cross herself, or utter charms against him.

Even so, when her mother asked him at dinner whether he had any family in England, she was conscious of a vague surprise that he should be possessed of anything so mundane as relations.

He had a girl cousin, he said; that was all.

'We don't like each other. She paints.'

'Is the painting a non-sequitur?' Walter asked.

'Oh, I like her painting well enough—what I've seen of it. It's just that we annoy each other, so we don't bother with one another.'

Lavinia asked what she painted; was it portraits?

Liz wondered, while they talked, if she had ever painted her cousin. It must be nice to be able to take a brush and a box of paints and put on record for one's own pleasure and satisfaction a beauty that could otherwise never belong to one. To have it to keep and look at whenever one wanted to until one died.

'Elizabeth Garrowby!' she said to herself. 'In no time at all you will be hanging up actor's photographs.'

But no; it wasn't like that at all. It was no more reprehensible than loving a—than admiring a work of Praxiteles. If Praxiteles had ever decided to immortalise a hurdler, the hurdler would have looked just like Leslie Searle. She must ask him sometime where he went to school, and if he had ever run races over hurdles.

She was a little sorry to see that her mother did not like Searle. No one would ever suspect it, of course; but Liz knew her mother very well and could gauge with micrometer accuracy her secret reactions to any given situation. She was aware now of the distrust that seethed and bubbled behind that bland front, as lava seethes and bubbles behind the smiling slopes of Vesuvius.

In that she was, of course, right. When Walter had borne his guest away to show him his room, and Liz had gone to tidy for dinner, Mrs Garrowby had catechised her sister about this unknown quantity that she had unloaded on the household.

'How do you know that he ever knew Cooney Wiggin at all?' she asked.

'If he didn't, Walter will soon find out,' Lavinia said reasonably. 'Don't bother me, Em. I'm tired. It was an awful party. Everyone screaming their heads off.'

'If his little plan is to burgle Trimmings, it will be too late tomorrow morning for Walter to find out that he didn't know Cooney at all. Anyone could say they knew Cooney. If it comes to that, anyone could say they knew Cooney and get away with it. There was practically no part of Cooney Wiggin's life that wasn't public property.'

'I can't think why you should be so suspicious about

him. We have often had people we didn't know anything about down here at a moment's notice——'

'Indeed we have,' Emma said grimly.

'And so far they have always been what they said they were. Why pick on Mr Searle for your suspicions?'

'He is much too personable to be wholesome.'

It was typical of Emma to shy at the word 'beauty', and to substitute a bastard compromise like 'personable'.

Lavinia pointed out that since Mr Searle was staying only till Monday the amount of unwholesomeness he could manage to disseminate was necessarily small.

'And if it is burglary you are thinking of, he's going to have a sad shock when he goes through Trimmings. I can't think, off-hand, of anything that is worth lugging as far as Wickham.'

'There's the silver.'

'Somehow I can't believe that anyone went to all the trouble of appearing at Cormac's party, and pretending to know Cooney, and asking for Walter, just to obtain possession of a couple of dozen forks, some spoons, and a salver. Why not just force a lock one dark night?'

Mrs Garrowby looked unconvinced.

'It must be very useful to have someone who is dead when you want to be introduced to a family.'

'Oh, Em,' Lavinia had said, breaking into laughter as much at the sentence as at the sentiment.

So Mrs Garrowby sat and brooded darkly behind her gracious exterior. She was not afraid for the Trimmings silver, of course. She was afraid of what she called the young man's 'personableness.' She distrusted it for itself, and hated it as a potential threat to her house.

3

BUT Emma did not, as Marta Hallard had prophesied, get the young man out of the house first thing on Monday morning. By Monday morning it was incredible to the inhabitants of Trimmings—all but Emma herself—that on the previous Friday they had never heard of Leslie Searle. There had never been any guest at Trimmings who had merged himself with the household as Searle did. Nor had there ever been anyone who intensified the life of each one of them to the same extent.

He walked round the farm with Walter, admiring the new brick paths, the piggery, and the separator. He had spent his school holidays on a farm, and was knowledge-able as well as receptive. He stood patiently in green lanes while Walter recorded in his little notebook a hedgerow sprout or a bird-note that would do for his broadcast next Friday. He photographed with equal enthusiasm the seventeenth-century honesty of the little farmhouse, and the surrealist irrelevance of Trimmings, and contrived to convey the essential quality of each. Indeed, his photographic comment on Trimmings was so witty that Walter after his involuntary laughter had a moment of discomfort. This amiable young man had more sides to him than were apparent in a discussion on husbandry. He had so taken for granted the boy's discipleship that it was as disconcerting to look at these photographs as if his shadow had suddenly spoken to him.

But he forgot the moment almost before it had passed. He was not an introspective person.

For the introspective Liz, on the other hand, life had become all of a sudden a sort of fun-fair. A kaleidoscope. A place where no surface ever stayed still or horizontal for more than a few seconds together. Where one was plunged into swift mock danger and whirled about in coloured lights. Liz had been falling in and out of love more or less regularly since the age of seven, but she had never wanted to marry anyone but Walter. Who was Walter, and different. But never in that long progression from the baker's roundsman to Walter had she been aware of anyone as she was aware of Searle. Even with Tino Tresca, of the yearning eyes and the tenor that dissolved one's heart like a melting ice, even with Tresca, craziest of all her devotions, it was possible to forget for minutes together that she was in the same room with him. (With Walter, of course, there was nothing remark-able in the fact that they should be sharing the same air: he was just there and it was nice.) But it was never possible to forget that Searle was in a room.

Why? she kept asking herself. Or rather, why not?

It had nothing to do with falling in love, this interest; this excitement. If, on Sunday night, after two days in his company, he had turned to her and said: 'Come away with me, Liz,' she would have laughed aloud at so absurd a notion. She had no desire to go away with him.

But a light went out of the room with him, and sprang

up again when he came back. She was aware of every movement of his, from the small mallet of his forefinger as it flicked the radio switch, to the lift of his foot as it kicked a log in the fireplace.

Why?

She had gone walking with him through the woods, she had shown him the village and the church, and always the excitement had been there; in his gentle drawling courtesy, and in those disconcerting grey eyes that seemed to know too much about her. For Liz, all American men were divided into two classes: those who treated you as if you were a frail old lady, and those who treated you as if you were just frail. Searle belonged to the first class. He helped her over stiles, and shielded her from the crowding dangers of the village street; he deferred to her opinion and flattered her ego; and, as a mere change from Walter, Liz found it pleasant. Walter took it for granted that she was adult enough to look after herself, but not quite adult enough to be consulted by Walter Whitmore, Household Word Throughout the British Isles and a Large Part of Overseas. Searle's was a charming reversal of form.

She had thought, watching him move slowly round the interior of the church, what a perfect companion he would have made if it were not for this pricking excitement; this sense of wrongness.

Even the unimpressionable Lavinia, always but semi-detached from her current heroine, was, Liz noticed, touched by this strange attraction. Searle had sat with her on the terrace after dinner on Saturday night, while Walter and Liz walked in the garden and Emma attended to household matters. As they passed below the terrace each time on their round of the garden, Liz could hear her aunt's light childlike voice babbling happily, like a little stream in the half-dark of the early moonrise. And on Sunday morning Lavinia had confided to Liz that no one had ever made her feel so *abandoned* as Mr Searle. 'I am sure that he was something very wicked in Ancient Greece,' she said. And had added with a giggle: 'But don't tell your mother that I said so!'

Against the entrenched opposition of her sister, her nephew, and her daughter, Mrs Garrowby would have found it difficult to rid Trimmings of the young man's presence; but her final undoing came at the hands of Miss Easton-Dixon.

Miss Easton-Dixon lived in a tiny cottage on the slope behind the village street. It had three windows, asymmetrical in their own right and in relation to each other, a thatched roof, and a single chimney, and it looked as if one good sneeze would bring the whole thing round the occupant's ears; but its aspect of disintegration was equalled only by its spick and span condition. The cream wash of the plaster, the lime-green paint of door and windows, the dazzling crispness of the muslin curtains, the swept condition of the red-brick path, together with the almost conscientious crookedness of everything that normally would be straight, made a picture that belonged by right to one of Miss Easton-Dixon's own fairytale books for Christmas.

In the intervals of writing her annual story, Miss Easton-Dixon indulged in handcrafts. In the schoolroom she had tortured wood with red-hot pokers. When pen-painting came in she had pen-painted with assiduity, and had graduated from that to barbola work. After a spell of sealing-wax, she had come to raffia, and thence to hand-weaving. She still weaved now and then, but her ingrained desire was not to create but to transform. No plain surface was safe against Miss Easton-Dixon. She would take a cold cream jar and reduce its functional simplicity to a nightmare of mock-Meissen. In times which have seen the disappearance of both the attic and the boxroom, she was the scourge of her friends; who, incidentally, loved her.

As well as being a prop of the Women's Rural Institute, a lavish provider of goods for bazaars, a devoted polisher of Church plate, Miss Easton-Dixon was also an authority on Hollywood and all its ramifications. Every Thursday she took the one o'clock bus into Wickham and spent the afternoon having one-and-ninepence-worth at the converted Followers of Moses hall that did duty as a cinema. If the week's film happened to be something of which she did not approve—a ukelele opus, for instance, or the tribulations of some blameless housemaid—she put the one-and-ninepence, together with the eight-penny bus fare, into the china pig on the mantelpiece, and used the fund to take her to Crome, when some film that she specially looked forward to was being shown in that comparative metropolis.

Every Friday she collected her *Screen Bulletin* from the newsagent in the village, read through the releases for the week, marked those she intended to view, and put away the paper for future reference. There was no bit player in two hemispheres that Miss Easton-Dixon could not give chapter and verse for. She could tell you why the make-up expert at Grand Continental had gone

33

over to Wilhelm's, and the exact difference that had made to Madeleine Rice's left profile.

So that poor Emma, walking up the spotless brick path to hand in a basket of eggs on her way to Evensong, was walking all unaware into her Waterloo.

Miss Easton-Dixon asked about the party to celebrate the birth of *Maureen's Lover* and Lavinia Fitch's literary coming-of-age. Had it been a success?

Emma supposed so. Ross and Cromarty's parties always were. A sufficiency of drink was all that was ever necessary to make a party a success.

'I hear that you have a very good-looking guest this weekend,' Miss Easton-Dixon said, less because she was curious than because it was against her idea of good manners to have gaps in the conversation.

'Yes. Lavinia brought him back from the party. A person called Searle.'

'Oh,' said Miss Easton-Dixon in absentminded encouragement, while she transferred the eggs to a tenpenny white bowl that she had painted with poppies and corn.

'An American. He says that he is a photographer. Anyone who takes photographs can say that he is a photographer and there is no one to deny it. It is a very useful profession. Almost as useful as "nurse" used to be before it became a matter of registration and reference books.'

'Searle?' Miss Easton-Dixon said, pausing with an egg in her hand. 'Not *Leslie* Searle, by any chance?'

'Yes,' said Emma, taken aback. 'His name is Leslie. At least that is what he says. Why?'

'You mean Leslie Searle is *here*? In Salcott St Mary? How simply unbelievable!'

34

'What is unbelievable about it?' Emma said, on the defensive.

'But he is *famous*.'

'So are half the residents of Salcott St Mary,' Emma reminded her tartly.

'Yes, but they don't photograph the most exclusive people in the world. Do you know that Hollywood stars go down on their knees to get Leslie Searle to photograph them? It is something that they can't buy. A privilege. An honour.'

'And, I take it, an advertisement,' said Emma. 'Are we talking about the same Leslie Searle, do you think?'

'But of course! There can hardly be two Leslie Searles who are American and photographers.'

'I see nothing impossible in that,' said Emma, a last-ditcher by nature.

'But of course it must be *the* Leslie Searle. If it won't make you late for Evensong we can settle the matter here and now.'

'How?'

'I have a photograph of him somewhere.'

'Of Leslie Searle!'

'Yes. In a *Screen Bulletin*. Just let me look it out; it won't take a moment. This really is exciting. I can't think of anyone more—more exotic—to find in Salcott of all places.' She opened the door of a yellow-painted cupboard (decorated Bavarian-fashion with scrolls of stylised flowers) and disclosed the neat stacks of hoarded *Bulletins*. 'Let me see. It must be eighteen months ago —or perhaps two years.' With a practised hand she thumbed down the edges of the pile, so that the date in the corner of each was visible for a moment, and picked two or three from the pile. 'There is a "contents" list on the outside of each,' she pointed out, shuffling them on the table, 'so it doesn't take a moment to find what one wants. So useful.' And then, as the required issue did not turn up at once: 'But if this is going to make you late, do leave it and come in on your way home. I shall look it out while you are in church.'

But nothing would now have moved Emma from the house until she had seen that photograph.

'Ah, here it is!' said Miss Easton-Dixon at last. ' "Lovelies And The Lens" it was called. I suppose one cannot expect style *and* information for threepence a week. However, if I remember rightly the article was more respect-worthy than the title. Here it is. These are samples of his work—that is a *very* clever one of Lotta Marlow, isn't it—and here, over the page, you see, is a self-portrait. Isn't that your weekend guest?'

It was a photograph taken at an odd angle and full of odd shadows; a composition rather than a 'likeness' in the old sense. But it was unmistakably Leslie Searle. The Leslie Searle who was occupying the 'tower' bedroom at Trimmings. Unless, of course, there were twins, both called Leslie, both called Searle, both Americans, and both photographers; which was something at which even Emma baulked.

She skimmed through the article, which, as Miss Easton-Dixon had indicated, was a perfectly straight-forward account of the young man and his work and might equally well have come out of *Theatre Arts Monthly*. The article welcomed him back to the Coast for his annual stay, envied him being free of the world for the rest of the year, and commended his new portraits of the stars, more especially that of Danny Minsky in Hamlet clothes. 'The tears of laughter that Danny has wrung from us have no doubt blinded us to that Forbes-Robertson profile. It took Searle to show us that,' they said.

'Yes,' said Emma, 'that's——' She had nearly said 'the creature' but stopped herself in time; 'that is the same person.'

No, she said cautiously, she did not know how long he was staying—he was Lavinia's guest—but Miss Easton-Dixon should certainly meet him before he left if that were humanly possible.

'If not,' said Miss Easton-Dixon, 'do please tell him how much I admire his work.'

But that, of course, Emma had no intention of doing. She was not going to mention this little matter at home at all. She went to Evensong and sat in the Trimmings pew looking placid and benevolent and being thoroughly miserable. The creature was not only 'personable', he was a personality, and by that much more dangerous. He had a reputation that for all she knew might vie with Walter's in worldly worth. He no doubt had money, too. It was bad enough when she had only his 'personableness' to fear; now it turned out that he was eligible as well. He had everything on his side.

If it had been possible to call up the powers of darkness against him, she would have done it. But she was in church and must use the means to hand. So she invoked God and all his angels to guard her Liz against the evils in her path; that is to say, against not inheriting Lavinia's fortune when the time came. 'Keep her true to Walter,' she prayed, 'and I'll——.' She tried to think of some bribe or penance that she could offer, but could think of

37

none at the moment, so she merely repeated: 'Keep her true to Walter,' with no inducement added and left it to the unselfish goodness of the Deity.

It did nothing to reassure her nor to bolster her faith in the Deity, to come on her daughter and Searle leaning on the little side gate into the Trimmings garden and laughing together like a pair of children. She came up behind them along the field path from the church, and was dismayed by some quality of loveliness, of youth, that belonged to their gaiety. A quality that was not apparent in any communion between Liz and Walter.

'What I like best is the yard or two of Renaissance before the bit of Border peel,' Liz was saying. They were evidently at their favourite game of making fun of the Bradford magnate's folly.

'How did he forget a moat, do you think?' Searle asked.

'Perhaps he started life digging ditches and didn't want to be reminded of them.'

'It's my guess he didn't want to spend money on digging a hole just to put water in it. They're Yankees, aren't they, up there?'

Liz 'allowed' that north-country blood had probably much in common with New England. Then Searle saw Emma and greeted her, and they walked up to the house with her, not self-conscious in her presence or stopping their game, but drawing her into it and sharing their delight with her.

She looked at Liz's sallow little countenance and tried to remember when she had last seen it so alive; so full of the joy of life. After a little she remembered. It was on a Christmas afternoon long ago, and Liz had experienced in the short space of an hour her first snow and her first Christmas tree.

So far she had hated only Leslie Searle's beauty. Now she began to hate Leslie Searle.

4

It was Emma's hope that Searle would go quietly away before any further evidences of desirableness were revealed to the family; but in that too she was bound to be frustrated. Searle had avowedly come to England for a holiday, he had no relations or intimate friends to visit, he had a camera and every intention of using it, and there seemed no reason why he should not stay at Trimmings and use it. His expressed intention, once he had seen the largely unspoiled loveliness of Orfordshire, was to find a good hotel in Crome and make that a centre for photographic foraging among the cottages and country houses of the neighbourhood. But that, as Lavinia swiftly pointed out, was absurd. He could stay at Trimmings, among his friends, and forage just as far afield and with as good results as he could at Crome. Why should he come back each night to a hotel room and the company of casual acquaintances in a hotel lounge, when he could return to a home and the comfort of his own room in the tower?

Searle would no doubt have accepted the invitation in any case, but the final makeweight was the suggestion that he and Walter might do a book together. No one could remember afterwards who first made the suggestion, but it was one that anyone might have made. It was from journalism that Walter had graduated to the eminence of radio commentator, and an alliance between one of Britain's best-known personalities and one of America's most admired photographers would produce a book that might, with luck, have equal interest for Weston-super-Mare and Lynchburg, Va. In partnership they could clean up.

So there was no question of Searle's departing on Monday morning, nor on Tuesday, nor on any specific day in a foreseeable future. He was at Trimmings to stay, it seemed. And no one but Emma found any fault with that arrangement. Lavinia offered him the use of her Rolls two-seater to take him round the country—it did nothing but lie in the garage, she said, when she was working—but Searle preferred to hire a small cheap car from Bill Maddox, who kept the garage at the entrance to the village. 'If I'm going nosing up lanes that are not much better than the bed of a stream, some of them, I want a car I don't have to hold my breath about,' he said. But Liz felt that this was merely a way of declining Lavinia's offer gracefully, and liked him for it.

Bill Maddox reported well of him to the village—'no airs at all and can't be fooled neither; upped with the bonnet and went over her as if he was bred to the trade' —so that by the time he appeared in the Swan with Walter of an evening Salcott St Mary knew all about him and were prepared to accept him in spite of his reprehensible good looks. The Salcott aliens, of course, had no prejudice against good looks and no hesitation whatever in accepting him. Toby Tullis took one look at him and straightway forgot his royalties, the new comedy he had just finished, the one he had just begun, and the infidelity of Christopher Hatton (how had he ever been such a half-wit as to trust a creature of a vanity so pathological that he could take to himself a name like that!) and made a bee-line for the bench where Walter had deposited Searle while he fetched the beer.

'I think I saw you at Lavinia's party in town,' he said, in his best imitation-tentative manner. 'My name is Tullis. I write plays.' The modesty of this phrase always enchanted him. It was as if the owner of a transcontinental railroad were to say: 'I run trains.'

'How do you do, Mr Tullis,' said Leslie Searle. 'What kind of plays do you write?'

There was a moment of silence while Tullis got his breath back, and while he was still searching for words Walter came up with the beer.

'Well,' he said, 'I see you have introduced yourselves.'

'Walter,' said Tullis, deciding on his line and leaning towards Walter with empressement, 'I have met him!'

'Met whom?' asked Walter who always remembered his accusatives.

'The man who never heard of me. I have met him at last!'

'And how does it feel?' asked Walter, glancing at Searle and deciding yet once again that there was more in Leslie Searle than met the eye.

'Wonderful, my boy, wonderful. A unique sensation.'

'If you care, his name is Searle. Leslie Searle. A friend of Cooney Wiggin.'

Walter saw a shadow of doubt cross the fish-grey eye of Toby Tullis and followed the thought quite clearly. If this beautiful young man had been a friend of the very-international Cooney, then was it possible that he had never heard of the even-more-international Toby

Tullis? Was it possible that the young man was taking him for a ride?

Walter set the beer mugs down, slid into the seat beside Searle, and prepared to enjoy himself.

Across the room he could see Serge Ratoff glaring at this new piece of grouping. Ratoff had at one time been the raison d'être and prospective star of an embryo play of Toby Tullis's which was to be called *Afternoon* and was all about a faun. Unfortunately it had suffered considerable changes in the processes of birth and had eventually become something called *Crépuscule*, which was all about a little waiter in the Bois, and was played by a newcomer with an Austrian name and a Greek temperament. Ratoff had never recovered from this 'betrayal'. At first he had drunk himself into scintillations of self-pity; then he had drunk to avoid the ache of self-pity that filled him when he was sober; then he was sacked because he had become independable both at rehearsals and performance; then he reached the ultimate stage of a ballet dancer's downfall and ceased even to practise. So that now, vaguely but surely, the fatty tissue was blurring the spare tautness. Only the furious eyes still had the old life and fire. The eyes still had meaning and purpose.

When Toby ceased to invite him to the house at Salcott, Ratoff had bought the old stable next the village shop; a mere lean-to against the shop's gable end; and made it into a dwelling for himself. This had proved in a quite unexpected way his salvation, for his point of vantage next the only shop in the place had turned him from a mere reject of Toby's into a general purveyor of gossip to the community, and therefore a person in his own

43

right. The villagers, lured by the childish quality in his make-up, treated him without the reservation that they used to the other aliens, employing to him the same tolerance that they used to their own 'innocents'. He was therefore the only person in the village who was equally free of both communities. No one knew what he lived on, or if he ever ate, as opposed to drinking. At almost any hour of the day he could be found draped in incorrigible grace against the post-office counter of the shop, and in the evenings he drank at the Swan like the rest of the community.

In the last few months a rapprochement had taken place between him and Toby, and there were rumours that he was even beginning to practise again. Now he was glaring at this newcomer to Salcott, this unsmirched unblurred radiant newcomer, who had taken Toby's interest. In spite of 'betrayal' and downfall, Toby was still his property and his god. Walter thought with a mild amusement how scandalised poor Serge would be if he could witness the treatment to which his adored Toby was being subjected. Toby had by now discovered that Leslie Searle was a fellow who photographed the world's celebrities, and was therefore confirmed in his suspicion that Searle had known quite well who he was. He was puzzled, not to say wounded. No one had been rude to Toby Tullis for at least a decade. But his actor's need to be liked was stronger than his resentment, and he was putting forth all his charm in an effort to win over this so-unexpected antagonist.

Sitting watching the charm at work, Walter thought how ineradicable was the 'bounder' in a man's personality. When he was a child his friends at school had used the word 'bounder' loosely to describe anyone who wore the wrong kind of collar. But of course it was not at all like that. What made a man a bounder was a quality of mind. A crassness. A lack of sensitivity. It was something that was quite incurable; a spiritual astigmatism. And Toby Tullis, after all those years, stayed unmistakably a bounder. It was a very odd thing. With the possible exception of the Court of St James's, there was no door in the world that was not wide open to Toby Tullis. He travelled like royalty and was given almost diplomatic privileges; he was dressed by the world's best tailors and had acquired the social tricks of the world's best people; in everything but essence he was the well-bred man of the world. In essence he remained a bounder. Marta Hallard had once said: 'Everything that Toby does is just a little off-key,' and that described it very well.

Looking sideways to see how Searle was taking this odd wooing, Walter was delighted to observe a sort of absentmindedness in Searle as he consumed his beer. The degree of absentmindedness was beautifully graded, Walter noticed; any more would have laid him open to the charge of rudeness and so put him in the wrong, any less might not have been obvious enough to sting Tullis. As it was, Toby was baffled into trying far too hard and making a fool of himself. He did everything but juggle with plates. That anyone should be unimpressed by Toby Tullis was a state of affairs not be be borne. He sweated. And Walter smiled into his beer, and Leslie Searle was gentle and polite and a little absentminded.

And Serge Ratoff continued to glare from the other side of the room.

Walter reckoned that he was two drinks short of making a scene, and wondered if they should drink up and go, before Serge joined them in a torrent of unintelligible English and unfathomable accusations. But the person who joined them was not Serge but Silas Weekley.

Weekley had been watching them from the bar for some time, and now brought his beer over to their table and greeted them. He came, as Walter knew, for two reasons: because he had a woman's curiosity, and because everything beautiful had for him the attraction of the repulsive. Weekley resented beauty, and it was not entirely to be held against him that he made a very large income indeed out of that resentment. His resentment was quite genuine. The world he approved of was, as Liz had said, 'all steaming manure and slashing rain'. And not even the clever parodies of his individual style had sufficed to ruin his vogue. His lecture tours in America were wild successes, not so much because his earnest readers in Peoria and Paduca loved steaming manure but because Silas Weekley looked the part so perfectly. He was cadaverous, and dark, and tall, and his voice was slow and sibilant and hopeless, and all the good ladies of Peoria and Paduca longed to take him home and feed him up and give him a brighter outlook on life. In which they were a great deal more generous than his English colleagues; who considered him an un-mitigated bore and a bit of an ass. Lavinia always referred to him as 'that tiresome man who always tells you that he was at a board school', and held that he was just a little mad. (He, on his part, referred to her as 'the woman Fitch', as one speaking of a criminal.)

Weekley had come over to them because he could not

46

keep away from the hateful beauty of Leslie Searle, and Walter caught himself wondering if Searle knew it. For Searle, who had been all gentle indifference with the eager Toby, was now engaged in throwing a rope over the antagonistic Silas. Walter, watching the almost feminine dexterity of it, was willing to bet that in about fifteen minutes Searle would have Silas roped and hogtied. He glanced at the big bland clock behind the bar and decided to time him.

Searle did it with five minutes to spare. In ten minutes he had Weekley, resentful and struggling, a prisoner in his toils. And the bewilderment in Weekley's sunken eyes was greater than ever the bewilderment in Toby's fish-scale ones had been. Walter nearly laughed aloud.

And then Searle put the final touch of comedy to the act. At a moment when both Silas and Toby were doing their rival best to be entertaining, Searle said in his quiet drawl: 'Do forgive. me, won't you, but I see a friend of mine,' and got up without haste and walked away to join the friend at the bar. The friend was Bill Maddox, the garage keeper.

Walter buried his face in his beer mug and enjoyed the faces of his friends.

It was only afterwards, rolling it over in his mind to savour it, that a vague discomfort pricked him. The fun had been so bland, so lightly handled, that its essential quality, its ruthlessness, had not been apparent.

At the moment he was merely amused by the typical reactions of Searle's two victims. Silas Weekley gulped down what was left of his beer, pushed the mug away from him with a gesture of self-disgust, and went out of the pub without a word. He was like a man fleeing from the memory of some frowsy back-room embrace; a man sickened by his own succumbing. Walter wondered for a moment if Lavinia could possibly be right, and Weekley was after all a little mad.

Toby Tullis, on the other hand, had never known either retreat or self-disgust. Toby was merely deploying his forces for further campaigning.

'A little farouche, your young friend,' he remarked, his eye on Searle as he talked to Bill Maddox at the bar.

Farouche was the last word that Walter would have used of Leslie Searle but he understood that Toby must justify his temporary overthrow.

'You must bring him to see Hoo House.'

Hoo House was the beautiful stone building that stood so unexpectedly in Salcott's row of pink and cream and yellow gables. It had once been an inn; and before that, it was said, its stones had been part of an abbey farther down the valley. Now it was a show-piece of a quality so rare that Toby, who normally changed his dwelling-place (one could hardly say his home) every second year, had refused all offers for it for several years now.

'Is he staying long with you?'

Walter said that he and Searle planned to do a book together. They had not yet decided on the form of it.

'Gipsying Through Orfordshire?'

'Something like that. I do the spiel and Searle does the illustrations. We haven't thought of a good central theme yet.'

'A little early in the year to go gipsying.'

'Good for photography, though. Before the county becomes clotted with greenery.'

'Perhaps your young friend would like to photograph

Hoo House,' Toby said, picking up the two mugs and moving with admirable casualness to the bar with them.

Walter stayed where he was and wondered how many drinks Serge Ratoff had had since last he noticed him. He had been only two short of a row then, he had reckoned. Now he must be almost at explosion point.

Toby put the mugs on the counter, entered first into conversation with the landlord, then with Bill Maddox, and so quite naturally with Searle again. It was dexterously done.

'You must come and see Hoo House,' Walter heard him say presently. 'It is very beautiful. You might even like to photograph it.'

'Has it not been photographed?' asked Searle, surprised. It was quite an innocent surprise; an astonishment that a thing so beautiful should be unrecorded. But what it conveyed to his hearers was: 'Is it possible that any facet of Toby Tullis's life has remained unpublicised?'

This was the spark that ignited Serge.

'*Yes!*' he shrieked, shooting out of his corner like a squib and sticking his furious small face within an inch of Searle's, 'it has been photographed! It has been photographed ten thousand times by the greatest photographers in the world and it does not need to be made cheap by any stupid amateur from a country that was stolen from the Indians even if he has a profile and dyed hair and no morals and a——'

'Serge!' said Toby, 'shut up!'

But the wild babble poured out of Serge's ravaged face without a pause.

'Serge! Do you hear! Stop it!' Toby said, and pushed

49

Ratoff lightly on the shoulder so as to urge him away from Searle.

This was the final touch, and Serge's voice rose into one high continuous stream of vituperation, most of it couched in mercifully unintelligible English but spattered liberally with phrases in French or Spanish and studded here and there with epithets and descriptions of a freshness that was delightful. 'You middle-west Lucifer!' was one of the better ones.

As Toby's hand took him by the back of the collar to drag him away from Searle by force, Serge's arm shot out to where Toby's new-filled beer mug was waiting on the counter. He reached it a split second before Reeve, the landlord, could save it, grabbed it, and launched the whole contents into Searle's face. Searle's head moved sideways by instinct, so that the beer streamed over his neck and shoulder. Screaming with baffled rage, Serge lifted the heavy mug above his head to fling it, but Reeve's large hand closed on his wrist, the mug was prised out of his convulsive clutch, and Reeve said: 'Arthur!'

There was no chucker-out at the Swan, since there had never been any need for one. But when any persuading had to be done, Arthur Tebbetts did it. Arthur was cattleman up at Silverlace Farm, and he was a large, slow, kind creature who would go out of his way to avoid treading on a worm.

'Come now, Mr Ratoff,' Arthur said, enveloping with his Saxon bulk the small struggling cosmopolitan. 'There's no call to get fussed over little things. It's that there gin, Mr Ratoff. I've told you afore. That ain't no drink for a man, Mr Ratoff. Now you come with me, and see if you don't feel the better of a dose of fresh air. See if you don't.'

Serge had no intention of going anywhere with anyone. He wanted to stay and murder this newcomer to Salcott. But there was never any successful argument against Arthur's methods. Arthur just put a friendly arm round one and leaned. The arm was like a limb of a beech tree, and the pressure was that of a landslide. Serge went with him to the door under pressure, and they went out together. Not for one moment had Serge stopped his torrent of accusation and offence, and not once as far as anyone knew had he repeated himself.

As the high babbling voice died into the outer air, the onlookers stirred into relief and conversation again.

'Gentlemen,' said Toby Tullis, 'I apologise on behalf of the Theatre.'

But it was not said lightly enough. Instead of being an actor's gay smoothing over of an awkward moment, it was Toby Tullis reminding them that he spoke for the English Theatre. As Marta had said: everything that Toby did was a little off-key. There was a murmur of amusement, but if anything his speech added to the village's embarrassment.

The landlord mopped Searle's shoulder with a glass-cloth, and begged him to come in behind and his missus would take some clean water to his suit and get the smell of the beer off it before it dried in. But Searle refused. He was quite amiable about it but seemed to want to get out of the place. Walter thought that he was looking a little sick.

They said good-evening to Toby, who was still explaining Serge's temperament in terms of the Theatre, and went out into the sweet evening.

'Does he often sound off like that?' Searle asked.

'Ratoff? He has made scenes before, yes, but never such a violent one. I've never known him use physical means before.'

They met Arthur, returning to his interrupted beer, and Walter asked what had become of the disturber.

'He run away home,' Arthur said with his large smile. 'Went off like an arrow from a bow. He could beat a hare, that one.' And went back to his drink.

'It's early for dinner yet,' Walter said. 'Let us walk home by the river and up by the field-path. I am sorry about the row, but I expect that in your job you are used to temperaments.'

'Well, I have been called things, of course, but so far nothing has actually been flung at me.'

'I dare swear no one ever thought of calling you a middle-west Lucifer before. Poor Serge.' Walter paused to lean on the bridge below the Mill House, and look at the reflection of the afterglow in the waters of the Rushmere. 'Perhaps the old saying is true and it is not possible to love and be wise. When you are as devoted to anyone as Serge is to Toby Tullis, I expect you cease to be sane about the matter.'

'Sane,' said Searle sharply.

'Yes; things lose their proper proportions. Which, I take it, is a loss of sanity.'

Searle was quiet for a long time, staring at the smooth water as it flooded so slowly towards the bridge and then was flicked under it with the sudden hysteria of water sucked round obstacles in its path.

'Sane,' he repeated, watching the place where the water lost control and was sucked under the culvert.

'I'm not suggesting the fellow is mad,' Walter said. 'He has just lost hold of common sense.'

'And is common sense so desirable a quality?'

'An admirable quality.'

'Nothing great ever came out of common sense' Searle said.

'On the contrary. Lack of common sense is responsible for practically every ill in life. Everything from wars to not moving up in the bus. I see there is a light in the Mill House. Marta must be back.'

They looked up at the pale bulk of the house glowing in the half-dark as a pale flower glows. A single light, still bright yellow in what was left of the daylight, starred the side that looked on the river.

'A light the way Liz likes them,' Searle said.

'Liz?'

'She likes them golden like that in the daylight. Before the dark turns them white.'

For the first time Walter was forced into considering Searle in relation to Liz. It had not crossed his mind until now to consider them in relation to each other at all, since he was not in the least possessive about Liz. This unpossessiveness might have been accounted to him for virtue if it had not sprung directly from the fact that he took her for granted. If by some method of hypnotism the last dregs of Walter's subconscious could have been dragged to the surface, it would have been found that he thought that Liz was doing very well for herself. Even the shadow of such a thought would have shocked Walter's conscious mind, of course; but since he was entirely unself-analytical and largely unselfconscious (a quality that enabled him to perpetrate the broadcasts

53

which so revolted Marta and endeared him to the British public), the farthest his conscious mind went was to hold it gratifying and proper that Liz should love him.

He had known Liz so long that she had no surprises for him. He took it for granted that he knew everything about Liz. But he had not known a simple little fact like her pleasure in lights in the daytime.

And Searle, the newcomer, had learned that.

And, what was more, remembered it.

A faint ripple stirred the flat waters of Walter's self-satisfaction.

'Have you met Marta Hallard?' he asked.

'No.'

'We must remedy that.'

'I have seen her act, of course.'

'Oh. In what?'

'A play called *Walk in Darkness*.'

'Oh, yes. She was good in that. One of her best parts, I think,' Walter said, and dropped the subject. He did not want to talk about *Walk in Darkness*. *Walk in Darkness* might be a Hallard memory, but it was one that held also Marguerite Merriam.

'I suppose we couldn't drop in now?' Searle said, looking up at the light.

'It's a little too near dinner time, I think. Marta isn't the kind of person you drop in on very easily. That, I suspect, is why she chose the isolated Mill House.'

'Perhaps Liz could take me down and present me tomorrow.'

Walter had nearly said: 'Why Liz?' when he remembered that tomorrow was Friday, and that he would be away all day in town. Friday was broadcast day. Searle had remembered that he would not be here tomorrow although he himself had forgotten. Another ripple stirred.

'Yes. Or we might ask her up to dinner. She likes good food. Well, I suppose we had better be getting along.'

But Searle did not move. He was looking up the avenue of willows that bordered the flat pewter surface of the darkening water.

'I've got it!' he said.

'Got what?'

'The theme. The connecting link. The motif.'

'For the book, you mean?'

'Yes. The river. The Rushmere. Why didn't we think of that before?'

'The river! Yes! Why didn't we? I suppose because it isn't entirely an Orfordshire river. But of course it is the perfect solution. It has been done repeatedly for the Thames, and for the Severn. I don't see why it shouldn't work with the smaller Rushmere.'

'Would it give us the variety we need for the book?'

'Indubitably,' said Walter. 'It couldn't be better. It rises in that hilly country, all sheep and stone walls and sharp outlines; then there's the pastoral bit with beautiful farm houses, and great barns, and English trees at their best, and village churches like cathedrals; and then Wickham, the essence of English market towns, where the villein that marched from the town cross to speak to King Richard in London is the same man that prods today's heifer on to the train on its way to the Argentine.' Walter's hand stole up to the breast pocket where he kept his notebook, but fell away again. 'Then the marshes.

You know: skeins of geese against an evening sky. Great cloudscapes and shivering grasses. Then the port: Mere Harbour. Almost Dutch. A complete contrast to the county at its back. A town full of lovely individual building, and a harbour full of fishing and coastwise traffic. Gulls, and reflections, and gables. Searle, it's perfect!'

'When do we start?'

'Well, first, how do we do it?'

'Will this thing take a boat?'

'Only a punt. Or a skiff where it widens below the bridge.'

'A punt,' Searle said doubtfully. 'That's one of those flat duck-shooting things.'

'Approximately.'

'That doesn't sound very handy. It had better be canoes.'

'Canoes!'

'Yes. Can you manage one?'

'I've paddled one round an ornamental pond when I was a child. That's all.'

'Oh, well, at least you've got the hang of it. You'll soon remember the drill. How far up could we start, with canoes? Man, it's a wonderful idea. It even gives us our title. "*Canoes on the Rushmere.*" A title with a nice swing to it. Like "*Drums Along the Mohawk.*" Or "*Oil for the Lamps of China*".'

'We shall have to tramp the first bit of it. The sheep-country bit. Down to about Otley. I expect the stream will take a canoe at Otley. Though, God help me, I don't anticipate being much at home in a canoe. We can carry a small pack from the source of the river—

it's a spring in the middle of a field, I've always understood—down to Otley or Capel, and from there to the sea we canoe. "*Canoes on the Rushmere*". Yes, it sounds all right. When I go up to town tomorrow I'll go and see Cormac Ross and put the proposition to him and see what he is moved to offer. If he doesn't like it, I have half a dozen more who will jump at it. But Ross is in Lavinia's pocket, so we might as well make use of him if he will play.'

'Of course he will,' Searle said. 'You're practically royalty in this country, aren't you!'

If there was any feeling in the gibe it was not apparent.

'I should really offer it to Debham's,' Walter said. 'They did my book about farm life. But I quarrelled with them about the illustrations. They were dreadful, and the book didn't sell.'

'That was before you took to the air, I infer.'

'Oh, yes.' Walter pushed himself off the bridge and began to walk towards the field-path and dinner. 'They did refuse my poems, after the farm book, so I can use that as a get-out.'

'You write poems too?'

'Who doesn't?'

'I for one.'

'Clod!' said Walter amiably.

And they went back to discussing the ways and means of their progress down the Rushmere.

5

'COME up to town with me and see Ross,' Walter said at breakfast next morning.

But Searle wanted to stay in the country. It was blasphemy, he said, to spend even one day in London with the English countryside bursting into its first green. Besides, he did not know Ross. It would be better if Walter put the proposition to Ross first, and brought him into the business later.

And Walter, though disappointed, did not stop to analyse the exact quality of his disappointment.

But as he drove up to town his mind was much less occupied than usual with the matter of his broadcast, and a great deal oftener than usual it strayed back to Trimmings.

He went to see Ross and laid before him the plans for *Canoes on the Rushmere*. Ross professed himself delighted and allowed himself to be beaten up an extra 2½ per cent on a provisional agreement. But of course nothing could be settled, he pointed out, until he had consulted Cromarty.

It was popularly supposed that Ross had taken Cromarty into partnership for the fun of it; as a matter of euphony. He had been doing quite well for himself as Cormac Ross, as far as anyone could judge, and there seemed on the surface no reason to rope in a partner;

more especially a partner as colourless as Cromarty. But Cormac Ross had sufficient West Highland blood in him to find it difficult to say no. He liked to be liked. So he engaged Cromarty as his smoke-screen. When an author could be received with open arms, the open arms were Cormac Ross's. When an author had regretfully to be turned down it was on account of Cromarty's intransigeance. Cromarty had once said to Ross in a fit of temper: 'You might at least let me *see* the books I turn down!' But that was an extreme case. Normally Cromarty did read the books that he was going to be responsible for rejecting.

Now, faced with the offer of a book by the British Public's current darling, Ross used the automatic phrase about consulting his partner; but his round pink face shone with satisfaction, and he bore Walter off to lunch and bought him a bottle of Romanée-Conti; which was wasted on Walter, who liked beer.

So, full of good burgundy and the prospect of cheques to come, Walter went on to the studio and his mind once more began to play tricks on him and run away back to Salcott instead of staying delightedly in the studio as was its habit.

For half of his weekly time on the air Walter always had a guest. Someone connected with the Open Air; a commodity in which Walter had lately taken so much stock as to make it a virtual Whitmore monopoly. Walter compèred the Open Air in the shape of a poacher, a sheep farmer from the back blocks of Australia, a bird watcher, a keeper from Sutherland, an earnest female who went round pushing acorns into roadside banks, a young dilettante who hunted with a hawk, and anyone else who happened to be both handy and willing. For the latter half of his time Walter merely talked.

Today his guest was a child who kept a tame fox, and Walter was dismayed to find himself disliking the brat. Walter loved his guests. He felt warm and protective and all-brothers-together about them; he never loved mankind so largely or so well as when he and his guests were talking together in his Half Hour. He loved them to the point of tears. And now it upset him to feel detached and critical about Harold Dibbs and his silly fox. Harold had a sadly under-developed jaw, he noticed, and looked regrettably like a fox himself. Perhaps the fox had stayed with him because it had felt at home. He felt guilty about having had this thought and tried to compensate by giving his voice more warmth than it would carry, so that his interest had a forced note. Harold and his fox were Walter's first failure.

Nor was the talk successful enough to blot out the memory of Harold. The talk was about 'What Earthworms do for England'. The 'for England' was a typical Whitmore touch. Other men might speak on the place of the Earthworm in Nature, and no one cared two hoots either about Nature or earthworms. But Walter pinned his worm on to a Shakespearean hook and angled gently with it, so that his listeners saw the seething legions of blind purpose turning the grey rock in the western sea into the green Paradise that was England. There would be fifty-seven letters tomorrow morning by the first available post from north of the Border, of course, to point out that Scotland too had her earthworms. But this was just so much additional evidence of Walter's drawing-power.

It was Walter's secret habit to speak to one particular

person when broadcasting; a trick which helped him to achieve that unselfconscious friendliness which was his trade-mark. It was never a real person; nor did he ever visualise his imaginary hearer in detail. He merely decided that today he would talk to 'an old lady in Leeds', or 'a little girl in hospital in Bridgwater', or 'a lighthouse-keeper in Scotland'. Today for the first time he thought of speaking to Liz. Liz always listened to his broadcast, and he took it for granted that she would listen, but his imaginary listener was so much a part of his act that it had never occurred to him before to use Liz as the person he talked to. Now, today, some obscure need to bind Liz closely to him, to make sure that she was there, blotted out his 'pretence' listener, and he talked to Liz.

But it was not the success it should have been. The mere recollection of Liz wooed his mind from the script, so that he remembered last night by the river, and the darkening willows, and the single golden star in the side of the Mill House. A daffodil-pale light, 'the way Liz liked them'. And his attention wandered from the worms and from England and he stumbled over the words, so that the illusion of spontaneity was lost.

Puzzled and a little annoyed, but still not greatly disturbed, he signed the autograph books that had been sent to the studio for that purpose, decided what was to be done in the case of (*a*) a request for his presence at a christening, (*b*) a request for one of his ties, (*c*) nineteen requests to appear on his programme, and (*d*) seven requests for financial loans; and turned his face home-wards. As an afterthought he turned back and bought a pound box of chocolate dragées for Liz. As he tucked it into the glove compartment it occurred to him that it must be some time since he took Liz something on his way home. It was a pleasant habit; he must do it more often.

It was only when the traffic dropped behind him, and the Roman directness of the arterial highway stretched uneventful in front of him that his mind went past Liz to the thing her image was hiding: Searle. Searle. Poor Serge's 'middle-west Lucifer'. Why Lucifer, he wondered? Lucifer, Prince of the Morning. He had always pictured Lucifer as a magnificent, burning figure six-and-a-half feet tall. Not at all like Searle. What in Searle had suggested Lucifer to Ratoff's accusing mind?

Lucifer. A fallen glory. A beauty turned evil.

He saw in his mind a picture of the Searle who walked round the farm with him; his hatless blond hair blown into untidy ends by the wind, his hands pushed deep into very English flannels. Lucifer. He nearly laughed aloud.

But there was, of course, a strangeness in Searle's good looks. A—what was it?—an unplaceable quality. Something not quite of the world of men.

Perhaps that was what had suggested fallen angels to Serge's fertile mind.

Anyhow, Searle seemed a good chap, and they were going to do a book together; and Searle knew that he was engaged to marry Liz, so that he would not——

He did not finish the thought, even to himself. Nor did it occur to him to wonder how a beauty that made one think of fallen angels was likely to affect a young woman engaged to a B.B.C. commentator.

He drove home at a better speed than normally, put away the car, took Liz's favourite sweets out of their place in the glove compartment, and went in to present them and be kissed for his forethought. He was also the bearer of the good news that Cormac Ross liked the idea of the book and was prepared to pay them well for it. He could hardly wait to reach the drawing-room.

The baronial hall was very silent and cold as he crossed it, and it smelled, in spite of anachronistic baize doors, of sprouts and stewed rhubarb. In the drawing-room, which as usual was warm and gay, there was no one but Lavinia, who was sitting with her feet on the fender and her lap covered with that day's issue of the highbrow weeklies.

'It's a strange thing,' said Lavinia, taking her nose out of the *Watchman*, 'how immoral it is to make money out of writing.'

'Hullo, Aunt Vin. Where are the others?'

'This rag used to worship Silas Weekley until he went and made himself a fortune. Em is upstairs, I think. The others aren't back yet.'

'Back? Back from where?'

'I don't know. They went out in that dreadful little car of Bill Maddox's after lunch.'

'After *lunch*.'

' "The slick repetition of a technique as lacking in subtlety as a poster." Don't they make you sick! Yes, I didn't need Liz this afternoon, so they went out. It has been a glorious day, hasn't it?'

'But it is only ten minutes till dinner time!'

'Yes. Looks as though they're going to be late,' said Lavinia, her eyes pursuing the slaughter of Silas.

So Liz hadn't heard the broadcast! He had been talking to her and she hadn't even been listening. He was dumbfounded. The fact that the old lady in Leeds, and the child in the hospital in Bridgwater, and the lighthouse-keeper in Scotland hadn't been listening either made no difference. Liz *always* listened. It was her business to listen. He was Walter, her fiancé, and if he spoke to the world it was right that she should listen. And now she had gone out gaily with Leslie Searle and left him talking into thin air. She had gone out gadding without a thought, on a Friday, on his broadcast afternoon, gone out God knew where, with Searle, with a fellow she had known only seven days, and they stayed out to the very last minute. She wasn't even there to have chocolates given her when he had gone out of his way to get them for her. It was monstrous.

Then the vicar arrived. No one had remembered that he was coming to dinner. He was that kind of man. And Walter had to spend another fifteen minutes with earthworms when he had already had more than enough of them. The vicar had listened to his broadcast and was enchanted by it; he could talk of nothing else.

Mrs Garrowby came in, greeted the vicar with commendable presence of mind, and went away to arrange for a supplement of tinned peas to the entrée and a pastry covering for the stewed rhubarb.

By the time that the missing pair were twenty minutes late and Mrs Garrowby had decided not to wait for them, Walter had changed his attitude and decided that Liz was dead. She would never be late for dinner. She was lying dead in a ditch somewhere. Perhaps with the car on top of her. Searle was an American and it was well-known that all Americans were reckless drivers and had no patience with English lanes. They had probably gone round a corner slap into something.

He played with his soup, his heart black with dread, and listened to the vicar on demonology. He had heard at one time or another everything that the vicar had to say on the subject of demonology, but at least it was a relief to get away from worms.

Just when his heart had blackened and shrunk to the state of a very old mushroom, the gay voices of Searle and Liz could be heard in the hall. They came in breathless and radiant. Full of off-hand apology for their lateness and commendation for the family in that they had not kept dinner back for them. Liz presented Searle to the vicar but did not think of casting any special word to Walter before falling on her soup like a starving refugee. They had been all over the place, they said; first they had viewed Twells Abbey, and adjacent villages; then they had met Peter Massie and had gone to look at his horses and given him a lift into Crome; then they had had tea at the Star and Garter in Crome, and they had been on the way home out of Crome when they found a cinema which was showing *The Great Train Robbery*, and it was of course not in anyone's power to refuse a chance of viewing *The Great Train Robbery*. They had had to sit through several modern exhibits before *The Great Train Robbery* appeared—which was what had made them late—but it had been worth waiting for.

An account of *The Great Train Robbery* occupied most of the fish course.

'How was the broadcast, Walter?' Liz said, reaching for some bread.

It was bad enough that she did not say: 'I am desolated to have missed your broadcast, Walter'; but that she should spare for the broadcast only the part of her mind that was not occupied with the replenishing of her bread plate was the last straw.

'The vicar will tell you,' said Walter. '*He* listened.'

The vicar told them, *con amore*. Neither Liz nor Leslie Searle, Walter noticed, really listened. Once, during the recital, Liz met Searle's glance as she passed him something and gave him her quick friendly smile. They were very pleased with themselves, with each other, and with the day they had had.

'What did Ross say about the book?' Searle asked, when the vicar had at last run down.

'He was delighted with the idea,' Walter said, wishing passionately that he had never begun this partnership with Searle.

'Have you heard what they plan, Vicar?' Mrs Garrowby said. 'They are going to write a book about the Rushmere. From its source to the sea. Walter is going to write it and Mr Searle to illustrate it.'

The vicar approved of the idea and pointed out its classic form. Was it to be on shanks's mare or with a donkey, he asked.

'On foot down to Otley, or thereabouts,' Walter said. 'And by water from there.'

'By water? But the Rushmere is full of snags in its early reaches,' the vicar said.

They told him about the canoes. The vicar thought canoes a sensible craft for a river like the Rushmere, but wondered where they could be got.

'I talked to Cormac Ross about that today,' Walter said, 'and he suggested that Kilner's, the small craft builders at Mere Harbour, might have some. They

66

build for all over the world. It was Joe Kilner who designed that collapsible raft-boat-tent that Mansell took up the Orinoco on his last trip, and then said afterwards that if he had thought in time he could have made it a glider too. I was going to suggest that Searle and I should go over to Mere Harbour tomorrow and see Kilner—if he has no other plans.'

'Fine,' Searle said. 'Fine.'

Then the vicar asked Searle if he fished. Searle did not, but the vicar did. The vicar's other interest, a short head behind demonology, was the dry fly. So for the rest of dinner they listened to the vicar on flies, with the detached interest that they might bring to cement-mixing, or gum-chewing, or turning the heel of a sock; a subject of academic interest only. And each of them used the unoccupied half of their minds in their own fashion.

Walter decided that he would leave the little white packet of chocolates on the hall table, where he had dropped it as he went in to dinner, until Liz asked about it; when he would tell her casually what it was. She would be full of compunction, he decided, that he had thought of her while she had entirely forgotten him.

As they walked out of the dining-room he glanced sideways to make sure that the little packet was still there. It certainly was. But Liz, too, it seemed, had dropped something on the table on her way in to dinner. A great flat box of candy from the most expensive confectioners in Crome. Four pounds weight at the very least. 'Confits,' it said in dull gold freehand across its cream surface, and it was tied up with yards of broad ribbon finished in a most extravagant bow. Walter considered the 'confits' affected and the ribbon deplorably ostentatious. The whole thing was in the worst of taste. So like an American to buy something large and showy. It made him quite sick to look at it.

What made him sick, of course, was not the box of candy.

He was sick of an emotion that was old before candy was invented.

As he poured brandy for Searle, the vicar and himself to drink with their coffee he looked round in his mind for comfort, and found it.

Searle might give her boxes of expensive sweetmeats, but it was he, Walter, who knew what her favourite sweets were.

Or—did Searle know that too? Perhaps the Crome confectioner didn't happen to have dragées.

He tilted the brandy bottle again. He needed an extra spot tonight.

6

IF Emma Garrowby could ever be said to be glad of any connection of Leslie Searle with Trimmings, she was glad of the plan for the book. It would take him away from the household for the rest of his stay in Orfordshire; and once the Rushmere trip was over he would go away and they would see no more of him. No harm had been done so far, that she could see. Liz liked being with the creature, of course, because they were both young and because they seemed to laugh at the same things and because, naturally, he was attractive to look at. But she showed no signs of being seriously attracted. She never looked at Searle unless she had something to say to him; never followed him with her eyes as girls in love did, never sat near him in a room.

For all her apprehensiveness, Emma Garrowby was an imperceptive woman.

It was the semi-detached Lavinia, oddly enough, who observed and was troubled. The trouble welled up and overflowed into words, almost against her will, some seven days later. She was dictating as usual to Liz, but was making heavy weather of it. This was so rare that Liz was puzzled. Lavinia wrote her books with great ease, being genuinely interested in the fate of her current heroine. She might not remember afterwards whether it was Daphne or Valerie who had met her

lover when she was gathering violets in the dawn on
Capri, but while Daphne (or Valerie) had been in the
process of that meeting and that gathering Lavinia
Fitch watched over her like a godmother. Now, contrary
to all precedent, she was distrait and had great difficulty
in remembering even what Sylvia looked like.

'Where was I, Liz, where was I?' she said, striding up
and down the room; a pencil stuck through the bird's-nest
mop of sandy hair and another being chewed to pulp
between her sharp little teeth.

'Sylvia is coming in from the garden. Through the
french window.'

'Oh, yes. "Sylvia paused in the window, her slim
form outlined against the light, her large blue eyes wary
and doubtful——" '

'Brown,' said Liz.

'What?'

'Her eyes.' Liz flipped back some pages of the script.
'Page 59. "Her brown eyes, limpid as rainpools lying on
autumn leaves——" '

'All right, all right. "——her large brown eyes wary
and doubtful. With a graceful movement of resolution
she stepped into the room, her tiny heels tapping lightly
on the parquet floor——" '

'No heels.'

'What d'you say?'

'No heels.'

'Why not?'

'She has just been playing tennis.'

'She could have changed, couldn't she?' Lavinia said
with a touch of asperity that was foreign to her.

70

'I don't think so,' Liz said patiently. 'She is still carrying her racket. She came along the terrace "swinging her racket lightly".'

'Oh. *Did* she!' Lavinia said explosively. 'I bet she can't even *play*! Where was I? "She stepped into the room—she stepped into the room, her white frock fluttering"—no; no, wait—"she stepped into the room"—Oh, *damn* Sylvia!' she burst out, flinging her chewed pencil on to the desk. 'Who cares what the silly moron does! Let her stay in the blasted window and starve!'

'What is the matter, Aunt Vin?'

'I can't concentrate.'

'Are you worried about something?'

'No. Yes. No. At least, yes, I suppose I am, in a way.'

'Can I help?'

Lavinia ran her fingers through the bird's-nest, found the pencil there, and looked gratified. 'Why, *there's* my yellow pencil.' She put it back again in her hair-do. 'Liz, dear, don't think me interfering or anything, will you, but you're not by any chance getting a little—a little *smitten* with Leslie Searle, are you?'

Liz thought how like her aunt it was to use an out-of-date Edwardianism like 'smitten'. She was always having to modernise Lavinia's slang for her.

'If by "smitten" you mean in love with him, be comforted. I'm not.'

'I don't know that that's what I do mean. You don't love a magnet, if it comes to that.'

'A what! What are you talking about?'

'It isn't a falling in love, so much. It's an attraction.

71

He fascinates you, doesn't he.' She made it a statement, not a question.

Liz looked up at the troubled childish eyes, and hedged. 'Why should you think that?' she asked.

'I suppose because I feel it too,' Lavinia said.

This was so unexpected that Liz had no words.

'I wish now I had never asked him down to Trimmings,' Lavinia said miserably. 'I know it isn't his fault—it isn't anything he *does*—but there's no denying that he is an upsetting person. There's Serge and Toby Tullis not on speaking terms——'

'That is nothing new!'

'No, but they *had* become friends again, and Serge was behaving quite well and working, and now——'

'You can hardly blame Leslie Searle for that. It would have happened inevitably. You know it would.'

'And it *was* very odd the way Marta took him back with her after dinner the other night and kept him till all hours. I mean the way she *appropriated* him as her escort, without waiting to see what the others were doing.'

'But the vicar was there to see Miss Easton-Dixon home. Marta knew that. It was natural that he should go with Miss Dixon; they live in the same direction.'

'It wasn't what she did, it was the way she did it. She —she *grabbed*.'

'Oh, that is just Marta's lordly way.'

'Nonsense. She felt it too. The—the fascination.'

'Of course, he is exceedingly attractive,' Liz said; and thought how utterly the cliché failed to convey any quality of Leslie Searle's.

'He is—uncanny,' Lavinia said, unhappily. 'There is

72

no other word. You wait and watch for the next thing he is going to do, as if it were—as if it were a sign, or a portent, or a revelation, or something.' She used the 'you' impersonally, but caught Liz's eye and said challengingly: 'Well, you *do*, don't you!'

'Yes,' Liz said. 'Yes, I suppose it is like that. As if—as if the smallest thing he does had significance.'

Lavinia picked up the chewed pencil from the desk and doodled with it on the blotter. Liz noticed that she was making figures-of-eight. Lavinia must be very troubled indeed. When she was happy she made herring-bones.

'It's very odd, you know,' Lavinia said, mulling it over in her mind. 'I get the same "kick" out of being in a room with him that I would get out of being in a room with a famous criminal. Only nicer, of course. But the same feeling of—of wrongness.' She made several furious figures-of-eight. 'If he were to disappear tonight, and someone told me that he was just a beautiful demon and not a human being at all, I would believe them. So help me, I would.'

Presently she flung the pencil back on to the desk, and said with a little laugh: 'And yet it's all so absurd. You look at him and try to find out what is so extraordinary about him, and what is there? Nothing. Nothing that can't be matched elsewhere, is there? That radiant fairness and that skin like a baby; that Norwegian correspondent of the *Clarion* that Walter used to bring down had those. He is extraordinarily graceful for a man; but so is Serge Ratoff. He has a nice gentle voice and an engaging drawl; but so have half the inhabitants of Texas and a large part of the population of Ireland.

You catalogue his attractions and what do they add up to? I can tell you what they *don't* add up to. They don't add up to Leslie Searle.'

'No,' said Liz soberly. 'No. They don't.'

'The—the *exciting* thing is left out. *What* is it that makes him different? Even Emma feels it, you know.'

'Mother?'

'Only it takes her the opposite way. She hates it. She quite often disapproves of the people I bring down, sometimes she even dislikes them. But she *loathes* Leslie Searle.'

'Has she told you so?'

'No. She didn't have to.'

No, thought Liz. She did not have to. Lavinia Fitch—dear, kind, abstracted Lavinia—manufacturer of fiction for the permanently adolescent, had after all a writer's intuition.

'I wondered for a while if it was that he was a little mad,' Lavinia said.

'Mad!'

'Only nor-nor-west, of course. There is an unholy attraction about people who are stark crazy in one direction but quite sane every other way.'

'Only if you know about their craziness,' Liz pointed out. 'You would have to know about their mental kink before you suffered any unholy attraction.'

Lavinia considered that. 'Yes, I suppose you are right. But it doesn't matter, because I decided for myself that the "mad" theory didn't work. I have never met anyone saner than Leslie Searle. Have *you*?'

Liz hadn't.

'You don't think, do you,' Lavinia said, taking to

doodling again and avoiding her niece's eye, 'that Walter is beginning to resent Leslie?'

'Walter,' Liz said, startled. 'No, of course not. They are the greatest friends.'

Lavinia, having with seven neat strokes erected a house, put the door in it.

'Why should you think that about Walter?' Liz said, challenging.

Lavinia added four windows and a chimney-stack, and considered the effect.

'Because he is so considerate to him.'

'Considerate! But Walter is *always*——'

'When Walter likes people he takes them for granted,' Lavinia said, making smoke. 'The more he likes them the more he takes them for granted. He even takes you for granted—as you have no doubt observed before now. Until lately he took Leslie Searle for granted. He doesn't any more.'

Liz considered this in silence.

'If he didn't like him,' she said at length, 'he wouldn't be doing the Rushmere with him, or the book. Well, would he?' she added, as Lavinia seemed wholly absorbed in the correct placing of a doorknob.

'The book is going to be very profitable,' Lavinia said, with only a hint of dryness.

'Walter would never collaborate with someone he didn't like,' Liz said stoutly.

'And Walter might find it difficult to explain why he didn't want to do the book after all,' Lavinia said as if she had not spoken.

'Why are you telling me this?' Liz said, half angry.

Lavinia stopped doodling and said disarmingly: 'Liz

darling, I don't quite know, except perhaps that I was hoping you would find some way of reassuring Walter. In your own clever way. Which is to say, without dotting any I's or crossing any T's.' She caught Liz's glance, and said: 'Oh, yes, you are clever. A great deal cleverer than Walter will ever be. He is not very clever, poor Walter. The best thing that ever happened to him was that you should love him.' She pushed the defaced blotter away from her and smiled suddenly. 'I don't think, you know, that it is entirely a Bad Thing that he should have a rival to contend with. As long as there is no chance of the contention becoming serious.'

'Of *course* it isn't serious,' Liz said.

'Then suppose we get that moron out of the window, and finish the chapter before lunch,' Lavinia said, and, picking up the pencil, began to chew on it again.

But a sense of shock stayed with Liz while she recorded, for the ultimate benefit of the lending libraries and the Inland Revenue, the doings of Sylvia the moron. It had not occurred to her that her awareness of Searle could be known to anyone but herself. Now it seemed that not only did Lavinia know very accurately how she felt about him, but she hinted that Walter too might know. But that surely was impossible. How could he know? Lavinia knew because, as she so frankly said, she too was a victim of the Searle charm. But Walter would have no such pointer to her emotions.

And yet Lavinia had been so right. Walter's first easy taking-for-granted attitude to the visitor *had* changed to a host and guest relationship. It had changed imperceptibly and yet almost overnight. When and why had it changed? There was the unfortunate coinciding of the two so-different boxes of sweets; but that could hardly have rankled in any adult mind. The buying of candy for a girl was an automatic reflex with Americans; of no more significance than letting her go first through a doorway. Walter could hardly have resented that. How then could Walter have guessed the secret that was shared only by her fellow sufferer, Lavinia?

Her mind went on to consider Lavinia and her perceptions. She considered the one count that Lavinia had left out of the indictment—the snubbing of Toby Tullis—and wondered whether Lavinia had not mentioned it because she did not know, or whether she was merely indifferent to any suffering that Toby might be subjected to. Toby, as the whole village knew, was enduring the finest tortures of frustration since Tantalus. Searle had refused, with the most unimaginably kind indifference, to go to see Hoo House, or to take part in any of the other activities that Toby was eager to arrange for him. He had even failed to show any interest when Toby offered to take him over to Stanworth and present him. This had never happened to Toby before. His freedom to trot in and out of the ducal splendours of Stanworth was his trump card. He had never before played it in vain. With Americans especially it took the trick. But not with this American. Searle wanted no part of Toby Tullis, and made it clear with the most charming good manners. He stonewalled with a grace that for all its mordant quality was delightful to watch. Intellectual Salcott watched it with open delight.

And it was that that excoriated Toby.

To be snubbed by Leslie Searle was bad enough; to have it known that he was snubbed was torture.

Truly, thought Liz, the advent of Leslie Searle had not been a particularly fortunate happening for Salcott St Mary. Of all the people whose lives he touched, only Miss Easton-Dixon, perhaps, was wholly glad of his coming. He had been lovely with Miss Dixon; as kind and patient with her endless questions as though he had been a woman himself and interested in the small talk of the film world. He had trotted out for her benefit all the light gossip of studio politics, and had exchanged with her reminiscences of films good and films bad until Lavinia had said that they were like a couple of housewives swapping recipes.

That was the night that Marta had come to dinner; and there had been a moment during that evening, when Liz, watching him with Miss Dixon, was seized with a terrible fear that she might after all be falling in love with Leslie Searle. She was still grateful to Marta for reassuring her. For it was when Marta commandeered him and carried him off with her into the night, and she felt no slightest pang at seeing them go, that she knew that, however strongly she felt Searle's attraction, she was in no bondage to him.

Now, recording the doings of Sylvia the moron, she decided that she would take Lavinia's advice and find some way of reassuring Walter, so that he went away on this trip happy and with no grudge against Searle in his heart. When they came back from Mere Harbour, where they were taking possession of the two canoes and arranging for their transport to Otley to await them there, she would think up some small exclusive thing to do with Walter; something that would be tête-à-tête. It had been too often a triangle lately.

Or too often, perhaps, the wrong tête-à-tête.

7

WALTER had welcomed the idea of progression by canoe, not because he looked forward to folding himself into an inadequate small boat, but, because it would give him his 'story'. If the book was to be a success he must have 'adventures', and an unusual method of locomotion was the easiest way of providing them. It is difficult to garner quaint experience when being borne along comfortably in a car. And walking has lost face since it became universal in the form of an activity called hiking. Walter, who had walked over a great part of Europe with a toothbrush and a spare shirt in his burberry pocket, would have been glad to do the Rushmere valley on foot, but felt that he could not hope to satisfy any modern devotee. His toothbrush-and-spare-shirt technique would merely puzzle the masochistic enthusiasts who plodded, packed and hobnailed, to the horizon their glazed eye was fixed on, more Atlas than Odysseus. And to do the valley as an incidental accompaniment to puppets or a Punch and Judy might be productive of copy but was a little infra dig. in one whose holding in the Open Air was of almost proprietorial dimensions.

So Walter welcomed the idea of a canoe. And in the last week or so he had begun to welcome the idea for a different reason altogether.

In a car or on foot he would be cheek by jowl with

Leslie Searle day after day; in a canoe he would be virtually free of him. Walter had reached the stage when the very sound of Searle's quiet drawl annoyed him into the need for momentary self-control. And a dim awareness that he was being a little ridiculous did nothing to soothe his annoyance. The last straw had been when Liz started being kind to him. He had never analysed Liz's attitude to him, which had always seemed an appropriate one. That is to say that Liz supplied the undemanding devotion that he considered ideal in a woman after eight months of Marguerite Merriam. And now Liz had gone kind on him. 'Condescending' was his private word for it. But for his new awareness of Liz he might not have noticed the change, but Liz had moved to the very forefront of his thoughts and he analysed her lightest word, her most fleeting expression. And so he caught her being kind to him. Kind! To *him*. To Walter Whitmore.

Nothing so revolutionary or so unbecoming could have happened but for the presence of Leslie Searle. Walter needed a great deal of self-control when he thought of Leslie Searle.

They had planned to camp out each night, weather permitting; and of this too Walter was glad. Not only would it give him opportunities for tangling the Great Bear in the branches of some oak, or describing the night life of field and stream, but it would excuse him from the close quarters of night in some tiny inn. You can stroll away by yourself from a bivouac, but not, without remark, from a pub.

The canoes were dubbed Pip and Emma—the Rushmere, according to Searle, being a place where it was always afternoon—and Mrs Garrowby was unreasonably annoyed to find that Searle owned the Emma one. But what dismayed her far more was a dawning realisation that she might not, after all, be getting rid of Searle. There was to be one piece of comparative cheating about the trip, it seemed. To photograph the larger pieces of landscape needed more apparatus than could conveniently be carried in a canoe that was already occupied by a sleeping-bag and groundsheet, so Searle was to come back later and photograph the set-pieces at his leisure.

But for all the subterranean tremors that agitated Trimmings—Lavinia's misgiving, Walter's resentment, Liz's feeling of guilt, Emma's hatred—life on the surface was smooth. The sun shone with the incongruous brilliance so common in England before the last trees are in leaf; the nights were windless and warm as summer. Indeed Searle, standing on the stone terrace after dinner one night, had pointed out that This England might very well be That France.

'Reminds you of Villefranche on a summer night,' he said. 'Until now that has been my measuring rod for magic. The lights on the water, and the warm air smelling of geranium, and the last boat out to the ship between one and two in the morning.'

'What ship?' someone had asked.

'Any ship,' Searle said lazily. 'I had no idea that Perfidious Albion had the magic too.'

'Magic!' Lavinia had said. 'Why, we're the original firm.'

And they laughed a little and were all friendly together.

And nothing disturbed that friendliness up to the moment when Walter and Searle departed together into the English landscape late on a Friday night. Walter had given his usual talk, had come home for dinner (always put back an hour and a half on 'talks' day) and they had all drunk to the success of *Canoes on the Rushmere*. Then Liz drove them through the sweet spring evening, up the valley of the Rushmere, to their starting-point twenty miles away. They were going to spend the night in Grim's House; a cave that overlooked the high pastures where the river originated. Walter said that it was apt and fitting that they should begin their tale in prehistoric England, but Searle doubted if the domestic arrangements were likely to be any more prehistoric than some he had already sampled. A lot of England, he said, didn't seem to have come far from Grim, whoever he was.

However, he was all for sleeping in a cave. He had slept, in his time, on the floor of a truck, on the open desert, in a bath, on a billiard table, in a hammock, and inside the cabin of a Giant Wheel at a fair, but so far he had not sampled a cave. He was all for the cave.

Liz took them to where the track ended, and walked up the hundred yards of grassy path with them to inspect their shelter for the night. They were all very gay, full of good food and good drink and a little drunk with the magic of the night. They dumped their food and sleeping bags, and walked Liz back to the car. When they stopped talking for a moment the quiet pressed against their ears, so that they stayed their steps to listen for some sound.

'I wish I wasn't going home to a roof,' Liz said into the silence. 'It's a night for the prehistoric.'

But she went away down the rutted track to the road,

her headlights making metallic green stains on the dark grass, and left them to the silence and the prehistoric.

After that the two explorers became mere voices on the telephone.

Each evening they rang up Trimmings from some pub or call-box to report progress. They had walked successfully down to Otley and found their canoes waiting for them. They took to the river and were delighted with their craft. Walter's first notebook was already full, and Searle was lyrical on the beauty of this England in its first light powdering of blossom. From Capel he called specially for Lavinia to tell her that she had been right about the magic; England did really have the original blue-print.

'They sound very happy,' Lavinia said in a half-doubtful, half-relieved way as she hung up. She longed to go and see them, but the compact was that they were to be as strangers in a strange land, passing down the river and through Salcott St Mary as though they had never seen it before.

'You spoil my perspective if you bring Trimmings into it,' Walter had said. 'I must see it as if I had never seen it before; the countryside, I mean; see it fresh and new.'

So Trimmings waited each night for their telephoned report; mildly amused at this make-believe gulf.

And then on Wednesday evening, five days after they had set out, they walked into the Swan and were hailed as the Stanleys of the Rushmere and treated to drinks by all and sundry. They were tied up at Pett's Hatch, they said, and were sleeping there; but they had not been able to resist walking across the fields to Salcott. By water it was two miles down river from Pett's Hatch to

Salcott, but thanks to the loop of the Rushmere it was only a mile over the fields from one to the other. There was no inn at Pett's Hatch, so they had walked by the field-path to Salcott and the familiar haven of the Swan.

Talk was general at first as each newcomer inquired as to how they did. But presently Walter took his beer to his favourite table in the corner, and after a little Searle followed him. Several times from then on one or other of the loungers at the bar made a movement towards the two to engage them once more in conversation, only to pause and change his mind as something in the attitude of the two men to each other struck him as odd. They were not quarrelling; it was just that something personal and urgent in their intercourse kept the others, almost unconsciously, from joining them.

And then, quite suddenly, Walter was gone.

He went without noise and without a goodnight. Only the bang of the door called their attention to his exit. It was an eloquent slam, furious and final; a very pointed exit.

They looked in a puzzled fashion from the door to the unfinished beer at Walter's empty place, and decided in spite of that angry sound that Walter was coming back. Searle was sitting at his ease, relaxed against the wall, smiling faintly; and Bill Maddox, encouraged by the easing of that secret tension that had hung like a cloud in the corner, moved over and joined him. They talked outboard-motors and debated clinker versus carvel until their mugs were empty. As Maddox got up to refill them he caught sight of the flat liquid in Walter's mug and said: 'I'd better get another for Mr Whitmore; that stuff's stale.'

'Oh, Walter has gone to bed,' Searle said.

'But it's only——' Maddox was beginning, and realised that he was about to be tactless.

'Yes, I know; but he thought it would be safer.'

'Is he sickening for something?'

'No, but if he stayed any longer he was liable to throttle me,' Searle said amiably. 'And at the school Walter went to they take a poor view of throttling. He is putting temptation behind him. Literally.'

'You been annoying poor Mr Whitmore?' said Bill, who felt that he knew this young American much better than he knew Walter Whitmore.

'Horribly,' Searle said lightly, matching a smile with Bill's.

Maddox clicked his tongue and went away to get the beer.

After that, conversation became general. Searle stayed until closing time, said goodnight to Reeve, the landlord, as he locked the door behind them, and walked down the village street with the others. At the narrow lane that led between the houses to the fields he turned off, pelted by their mock-condolences on his lack of a snug bed, and throwing back in his turn accusations of frowst and ageing arteries.

'Goodnight!' he called, from far down the lane.

And that was the last that anyone in Salcott St Mary ever saw of Leslie Searle.

Forty-eight hours later Alan Grant stepped back into the affairs of the Trimmings household.

8

GRANT had just come back from Hampshire, where a case had ended unhappily in suicide, and his mind was still reviewing the thing, wondering how he might have managed things differently to a different end; so that he listened with only an ear-and-a-half to what his superior was saying to him until a familiar name caught his whole attention.

'Salcott St Mary!' said Grant.

'Why?' said Bryce, stopping his account. 'Do you know the place?'

'I've never been there, but I know of it, of course.'

'Why of course?'

'It's a sort of artistic thieves'-kitchen. There's been a migration of intelligentsia to the place. Silas Weekley lives there, and Marta Hallard, and Lavinia Fitch. Tullis has a house there too. It isn't Toby Tullis who is missing, by any chance?' he asked hopefully.

'No, unfortunately. It's a chap called Searle. Leslie Searle. A young American, it seems.'

For a moment Grant was back in the crowded doorway of Cormac Ross's room, listening to a voice saying: 'I've forgotten my megaphone.' So the beautiful young man had disappeared.

'Orfordshire say they want to put it in our laps not because they think the problem is insoluble but because it's a kid-glove affair. They think it would be easier for us than for them to pursue inquiries among the local bigwigs, and if there is any arresting to be done they would rather that we did it.'

'Arresting? Are they suggesting that it was murder?'

'They have a strong leaning to that theory, I understand. But, as the local inspector said to me, it sounds so absurd when you say it aloud that they shrink from uttering the name, even.'

'What name?'

'Walter Whitmore.'

'*Walter Whitmore!*' Grant let out his breath in a soundless whistle. 'I don't wonder they don't like saying it aloud. Walter Whitmore! What is he supposed to have done to Searle?'

'They don't know. All they've got is some suggestion of a quarrel before the disappearance. It seems that Walter Whitmore and Searle were travelling down the Rushmere in canoes, and——'

'Canoes?'

'Yes, a kind of stunt. Whitmore was going to write about it and this chap Searle was going to supply the illustrations.'

'Is he an artist, then?'

'No. A photographer. They camped out each night, and on Wednesday night they were sleeping on the river bank about a mile from Salcott. They both came to the pub at Salcott for a drink that evening. Whitmore left early—in some sort of pet, it is alleged. Searle stayed till closing-time and was seen to start off down the track to the river. After that he was not seen by anyone.'

'Who reported the disappearance?'

'Whitmore did next morning. When he woke and found that Searle had not occupied his sleeping-bag.'

'He didn't see Searle at all on Wednesday night after leaving the pub?'

'No, he says he fell asleep, and though he woke in the night he took it for granted that Searle had come back and was sleeping; it was too dark to see anything. It was only when daylight came that he realised that Searle had not been to bed.'

'The theory is that he fell into the river, I suppose.'

'Yes. The Wickham people took charge and dragged for a body. But it's a bad, muddy stream, there, between Capel and Salcott St Mary, the Wickham people say, so they weren't unbearably surprised not to find one.'

'I don't wonder they don't want to touch the business,' Grant said dryly.

'No. It's a delicate affair. No real suggestion of anything but accident. And yet—one big question mark.'

'But—but *Walter Whitmore*!' Grant said. 'There *is* something inherently absurd about it, you know. What would that lover of little bunnies have to do with murder?'

'You've been in the Force long enough to know that it is just those lovers of little bunnies that commit murder,' his chief said snappily. 'Anyhow, it is going to be your business to sift this artistic thieves'-kitchen of yours through a fine-mesh riddle until you're left with something that won't go through the mesh. You had better take a car. Wickham say it is four miles from a station, with a change at Crome anyhow.'

'Very good. Do you mind if I take Sergeant Williams with me?'

'As chauffeur, or what?'

89

'No,' Grant said amiably. 'Just so that he knows the lay-out. Then if you pull me off this for something more urgent—as you will at any moment—Williams can carry on.'

'You do think up the most convincing excuses for snoozing in a car.'

Grant took this, rightly, as capitulation, and went away to collect Williams. He liked Williams and liked working with him. Williams was his opposite and his complement. He was large and pink and slow-moving, and he rarely read anything but an evening paper; but he had terrier qualities that were invaluable in a hunt. No terrier at a rat hole ever displayed more patience or more pertinacity than Williams did when introduced to a quarry. 'I would hate to have you on my tail,' Grant had said to him more than once in their years of working together.

To Williams, on the other hand, Grant was everything that was brilliant and spontaneous. He admired Grant with passion, and envied him without malice; Williams had no ambition, and coveted no man's shoes. 'You've no idea how lucky you are, sir,' Williams would say, 'not looking like a policeman. Me, I go into a pub, and they take one look at me and think: Copper! But with you, they just cast an eye over you and think: Army in plain clothes; and they don't think another thing about you. It's a great advantage in a job like ours, sir.'

'But you have advantages that I lack, Williams,' Grant had once pointed out.

'As what, for instance?' Williams had said, unbelieving.

'You have only to say: "Hop it!" and people just dissolve. When I say "Hop it!" to anyone, they are as likely as not to say: "Who do you think you're talking to?"'

'Lord love you, sir,' Williams had said. 'You don't even have to say: "Hop it!" You just look at them, and they begin to recollect appointments.'

Grant had laughed and said: 'I must try that sometime!' But he enjoyed Williams's mild hero-worship; and still more he enjoyed his reliability and his persistence.

'Do you listen to Walter Whitmore, Williams?' he asked, as Williams drove him down the unswerving road that the Legions had first surveyed two thousand years ago.

'Can't say I do, sir. I'm not one for the country, much. Being born and brought up in it is a drawback.'

'A drawback?'

'Yes. You know just how workaday it really is.'

'More Silas Weekley than Walter Whitmore.'

'I don't know about the Silas bloke, but it certainly isn't like anything Walter Whitmore makes of it.' He thought of it for a little. 'He's a dresser-upper,' he said. 'Look at this Rushmere trip.'

'I'm looking.'

'I mean, there wasn't anything to prevent him staying at home with his aunt and doing the river valley like a Christian, in a car. The Rushmere isn't all that long. But no, he has to frill it up with a canoe and things.'

Mention of Walter's aunt prompted Grant to another question.

'I suppose you don't read Lavinia Fitch?'

'No, but Nora does.'

Nora was Mrs Williams, and the mother of Angela and Leonard.

'Does she like them?'

'Loves them. She says three things make her feel cosy in advance. A hot-water bottle, a quarter-pound of chocolates, and a new Lavinia Fitch.'

'If Miss Fitch did not exist, it seems, it would be necessary to invent her,' Grant said.

'Must make a fortune,' said Williams. 'Is Whitmore her heir?'

'Her presumptive heir, at any rate. But it isn't Lavinia who has disappeared.'

'No. What could Whitmore have against this Searle chap?'

'Perhaps he just objects to fauns on principle.'

'To what, sir?'

'I saw Searle once.'

'You did!'

'I spoke to him in passing at a party about a month ago.'

'What was he like, sir?'

'A very good-looking young man indeed.'

'Oh,' Williams said, in a thoughtful way.

'No,' said Grant.

'No?'

'American,' Grant said irrelevantly. And then, remembering that party, added: 'He seemed to be interested in Liz Garrowby, now that I remember.'

'Who is Liz Garrowby?'

'Walter Whitmore's fiancée.'

'He was? Well!'

'But don't go making five of it until we get some evidence. I can't believe that Walter Whitmore ever had enough red blood in him to conk anyone on the head and push them into a river.'

'No,' Williams said, considering it. 'Come to think of it, he's more of a push-ee.'

Which put Grant in a good mood for the rest of the journey.

At Wickham they were welcomed by the local inspector, Rodgers; a thin, anxious individual who looked as though he slept badly. He was alert, however, and informative and full of forethought. He had even booked two rooms at the Swan in Salcott and two at the White Hart in Wickham, so that Grant could have his choice. He bore them off to lunch at the White Hart, where Grant confirmed the room-booking and caused the Salcott booking to be cancelled. There was to be no suggestion yet that Scotland Yard were interested in the matter of Leslie Searle's disappearance; and it was not possible to conduct inquiries from the Swan without creating a sensation in Salcott.

'I'd like to see Whitmore, though,' Grant said. 'I suppose he is back at—what do you call it: Miss Fitch's place.'

'Trimmings. But he's up in town today giving his broadcast.'

'In London?' said Grant, a little surprised.

'It was arranged like that before they set out on this trip. Mr Whitmore's contract calls for a month off in August, when broadcasting has its "off" season; so there was no question, it seems, of passing up this week's broadcast just because he was canoeing on the Rushmere. They had arranged to be in Wickham today and to spend the night there. They had booked two rooms at the Angel. It's the olde-worlde show-place in Wickham. Very photogenic. Then this happened. But since there was nothing Mr Whitmore could do here, he went up to do his half-hour, just as he would have if they had reached Wickham.'

'I see. And he is coming back tonight?'

'If he doesn't vanish into thin air.'

'About this vanishing: did Whitmore agree that there had been disagreement between them?'

'I didn't put it to him. That's what——' The Inspector broke off.

'That's what I'm here for,' Grant said, finishing the sentence for him.

'That's about it, sir.'

'Where did the "disagreement" story come from?'

'The Swan. Everyone who was there on Wednesday night had the impression that there was some kind of tension between them.'

'No overt quarrel?'

'No, nothing like that. If there had been anything like that I could have taxed him with it. All that happened was that Mr Whitmore left early without saying goodnight, and Searle said he was angry about something.'

'*Searle* said! To whom?'

'To the local garage-keeper. A chap called Maddox. Bill Maddox.'

'Have you talked to Maddox?'

'I talked to them all. I was in the Swan last night. We spent the day dragging the river in case he had fallen in, and making inquiries all round the neighbourhood in case he had lost his memory and was just wandering. We couldn't find any body, and no one had seen him or anyone answering his description. So I finished up at the Swan, and saw most of the people who had been there on Wednesday night. It's the only pub in the place, and a very nice respectable little house run by a Joey; an ex-sergeant of Marines; and it's the meeting-place for the whole village. None of them was exactly anxious to involve Mr Whitmore——'

'Popular, is he?'

'Well, popular enough. He probably shines by comparison. There's a very odd crew lives here, I don't know if you know.'

'Yes, I've heard.'

'So they didn't want to get Walter Whitmore into trouble, but they had to explain why the two friends didn't go back to their camp together. And once they broke down and talked they were unanimous that there was some sort of trouble between them.'

'Did this Maddox volunteer his story?'

'No, the local butcher did. Maddox had told them about it on the way home on Wednesday. After they had seen Searle go away by himself down the lane. Maddox confirmed it, though.'

'Well, I'll go and see Whitmore when he comes back tonight, and ask for his story. Meanwhile we'll go and see the place where they camped on Wednesday night.'

9

'I DON'T want to appear in Salcott just yet,' Grant said as they drove out of Wickham. 'Is there some other way to the river bank?'

'There's no way at all to the river bank, properly speaking. There's about a mile of field-path from Salcott to where they were. But we could reach the place just as easily from the main Wickham-Crome road, across the fields. Or we could turn off the road by a lane that goes to Pett's Hatch, and walk down the river bank from there. They were moored about a quarter mile below Pett's Hatch.'

'On the whole, I'd rather walk across the fields from the main road. It would be interesting to see how much of a walk it is. What kind of a village is Pett's Hatch?'

'It isn't a village at all. Just a ruined mill and the few cottages that used to house the workers there. That is why Whitmore and Searle walked into Salcott for their evening drink.'

'I see.'

The ever-efficient Rodgers pulled a one-inch Survey map out of the pocket of his car, and studied it. The field opposite which they had stopped looked to Grant's urban eye exactly like any other field that they had passed since leaving Wickham, but the Inspector said:

'It should be about opposite here, I think. Yes; there's where they were; and here is us.'

He showed the lay-out to Grant. North and south ran the road from Wickham south to Crome. West of it lay the Rushmere, out of sight in its valley, running north-east to meet the road at Wickham. At a point level with where they were now halted, the river ran back on itself in a wide loop over the flat bed of the valley. At the point where it first curved back, Whitmore and Searle had made their camp. On the farther side of the valley, where the river came back level with them, was Salcott St Mary. Both their camp and the village of Salcott were on the right bank of the river, so that only a short mile of alluvial land lay between their camp and the village.

As the three men reached the third field from the road, the countryside opened below them, so that the relevant section of the Rushmere valley was laid out for them as it had been on Rodgers's map: the flat green floor with the darker green scarf of the Rushmere looped across it, the huddle of roofs and gardens on the far side where Salcott St Mary stood in its trees; the lonely cluster, back up the river to the south, that was Pett's Hatch.

'Where is the railway from here?' Grant asked.

'There is no railway nearer than Wickham. No station, that is. The line runs the other side of the Wickham-Crome road; not in the valley at all.'

'Plenty of buses on the Wickham-Crome road?'

'Oh, yes. But you're not suggesting that the fellow just ducked, are you?'

'I'm keeping the possibility in mind. After all, we know nothing about him. I'll admit there are more likely possibilities.'

97

Rodgers led them down the long slope to the river bank. Where the river turned away south-west two large trees broke the line of pollarded willows: a tall willow and an ash. Under the ash were moored two canoes. The grass still had a trampled look.

'This is the place,' Rodgers said. 'Mr Whitmore spread his sleeping-bag under that big willow, and Searle put his round the other side of the ash where there is a hollow between the roots that makes a natural shelter. So that it was quite natural that Mr Whitmore should not know that he wasn't there.'

Grant moved over to where Searle's bed had been, and considered the water.

'How much current is there? If he had tripped over those roots in the dark and taken a header into the river, what would happen?'

'It's a horrid stream, the Rushmere, I admit. All pot-holes and under-tows. And a bottom of what the Chief Constable calls "immemorial mud". But Searle could swim. Or so Walter Whitmore says.'

'Was he sober?'

'Cold, stone sober.'

'Then if he went into the water unconscious, where would you expect to find his body?'

'Between here and Salcott. Depends on the amount of rain. We've had so little lately that you'd normally find the river low, but they had a cloudburst at Tunstall on Tuesday—out of the blue in the good old English fashion—and the Rushmere came down like a mill-race.'

'I see. What became of the camp stuff?'

'Walter Whitmore had it taken up to Trimmings.'

'I take it that Searle's normal belongings are still at Trimmings.'

'I expect so.'

'Perhaps I had better take a look through them tonight. If there was anything interesting to us among them it will have gone by now, but they may be suggestive. Had Searle been on good terms with the other inhabitants of Salcott, do you know?'

'Well, I hear there was a scene about a fortnight ago. A dancer chap flung a mug of beer over him.'

'Why?' asked Grant, identifying the 'dancer chap' without difficulty. Marta was a faithful recorder of Salcott history.

'He didn't like the attentions that Toby Tullis was paying to Searle, so they say.'

'Did Searle?'

'No, if all reports are true,' Rodgers said, his anxious face relaxing to a moment's amusement.

'So Tullis wouldn't love him very much either?'

'Perhaps not.'

'You haven't had time, I suppose, to get round to alibis.'

'No. It wasn't until early evening that we found it might be more than a simple case of missing. Up till then it was a simple matter of drag and search. When we found what was turning up we wanted outside help and sent for you.'

'I'm glad you sent so soon. It's a great help to be there when the tapes go up. Well, I don't think there is anything else we can do here. We had better get back to Wickham, and I'll take over.'

Rodgers dropped them at the White Hart, and left

them with assurances of any help that was within his power.

'Good man, that,' Grant said, as they climbed the stairs to inspect their rooms under the roof—rooms with texts in wools and flowered wall-paper—'he ought to be at the Yard.'

'It's a queer set-up, isn't it?' Williams said, firmly taking the pokier of the two rooms. 'The rope trick in an English meadow. What do you think happened to him, sir?'

'I don't know about "rope trick", but it does smell strongly of sleight-of-hand. Now you see it, now you don't. The old conjurer's trick of the distracted attention. Ever seen a lady sawn in half, Williams?'

'Many's the time.'

'There's a strong aroma of sawn lady about this. Or don't you smell it?'

'I haven't got your nose, sir. All I see is a very queer set-up. A spring night in England, and a young American goes missing in the mile between the village and the river. You really think he *might* have ducked, sir?'

'I can't think of any adequate reason why he should, but perhaps Whitmore can.'

'I expect he will be very anxious to,' Williams said dryly.

But oddly enough Walter Whitmore showed no anxiety to put forward any such theory. On the contrary, he scorned it. It was absurd, he said, manifestly absurd, to suggest that Searle should have left of his own accord. Quite apart from the fact that he was very happy, he had a very profitable deal to look forward to. He had been enormously enthusiastic about the book they were doing together, and it was fantastic to suggest that he would just walk out like that.

Grant had come to Trimmings after dinner, tactfully allowing for the fact that dinner at Trimmings must be very late on broadcast day. He had sent in word to ask if Mr Whitmore would see Alan Grant, and had not mentioned his business until he was face to face with Walter.

His first thought on seeing Walter Whitmore in the flesh was how much older he looked than he had expected; and then wondered whether it was that Walter looked much older than he had done on Wednesday. He looked disorientated, Grant thought; adrift. Something had happened to him that did not belong to the world he knew and recognised.

But he took Grant's announcement of his identity calmly. 'I was almost expecting you,' he said, offering cigarettes. 'Not you personally, of course. Just a representative of what has come to be known as the Higher Levels.'

Grant had asked about their trip down the Rushmere, so as to set him talking; if you got a man to talk enough he lost his defensive quality. Whitmore was drawing too hard on his cigarette but talking quite freely. Before he had actually reached their Wednesday evening visit to the Swan, Grant deflected him. It was too early yet to ask him about that night.

'You don't really know much about Searle, do you,' he pointed out. 'Had you heard of him at all before he turned up at that party of Ross's?'

'No, I hadn't. But that isn't strange. Photographers are two a penny. Almost as common as journalists. There was no reason why I should have heard of him.'

'You have no reason to believe that he may not be what he represented himself to be?'

'No, certainly not. I may never have heard of him, but Miss Easton-Dixon certainly had.'

'Miss Easton-Dixon?'

'One of our local authors. She writes fairy-tales, and is a film addict. Not only did she know about Searle but she has a photograph.'

'A photograph?' Grant said, startled and pleased.

'In one of those film magazines. I haven't seen it myself. She talked about it one night when she came to dinner.'

'And she met Searle when she came to dinner? And identified him?'

'She did. They had a wonderful get-together. Searle had photographed some of her pet actors, and she had reproductions of them too.'

'So there is no doubt in your mind that Searle is what he says he is.'

'I notice you use the present tense, Inspector. That cheers me.' But he sounded more ironic than cheered.

'Have you yourself any theory as to what could have happened, Mr Whitmore?'

'Short of fiery chariots or witches' broomsticks, no. It is the most baffling thing.'

Grant caught himself thinking that Walter Whitmore, too, was moved to think of sleight-of-hand.

'The most reasonable explanation, I suppose,' Walter went on, 'is that he lost his way in the dark and fell into the river at some other spot, where no one would hear him.'

'And why don't you approve of that theory?' Grant asked, answering the tone that Whitmore used.

'Well, for one thing, Searle had eyes like a cat. I had slept out with him for four nights, and I know. He was wonderful in the dark. Secondly he had an extra-good bump of locality. Thirdly he was by all accounts cold sober when he left the Swan. Fourthly it is a bee-line from Salcott to the river-bank where we were camped, by the hedges all the way. You can't stray, because if you walk away from the hedge you walk into plough or crop of some kind. And lastly, though this is hearsay evidence, Searle could swim very well indeed.'

'There is a suggestion, Mr Whitmore, that you and Searle were on bad terms on Wednesday evening. Is there any truth in that?'

'I thought we should get to that sooner or later,' Walter said. He pressed the half-smoked cigarette into the ashtray until it was a misshapen wreck.

'Well?' Grant prompted, as he seemed to have nothing more to say.

'We had what might be called a—a "spat", I suppose. I was—annoyed. Nothing more than that.'

'He annoyed you so much that you left him at the pub and walked back by yourself.'

'I like being by myself.'

'And you went to sleep without waiting for his return.'

'Yes. I didn't want to talk to him any more that night. He annoyed me, I tell you. I thought that I might be in a better humour and he in a less provocative mood in the morning.'

'He was provocative?'

'I think that is the word.'

'About what?'

'I don't have to tell you that.'

'You don't have to tell me anything, Mr Whitmore.'

'No, I know I don't. But I want to be as helpful as I can. God knows I want this thing cleared up as soon as possible. It is just that what we—disagreed about is something personal and irrelevant. It has no bearing whatever on anything that happened to Searle on Wednesday night. I certainly didn't lie in wait for him on the way home, or push him into the river, or subject him to violence.'

'Do you know of anyone who would be likely to want to?'

Whitmore hesitated; presumably with Serge Ratoff in his mind.

'Not that kind of violence,' he said at length.

'Not what kind?'

'Not that waiting-in-the-dark kind.'

'I see. Just the ordinary sock-in-the-jaw kind. There was a scene with Serge Ratoff, I understand.'

'Anyone who gets through life in close proximity to Serge Ratoff and doesn't have a scene with him must be abnormal,' Walter said.

'You don't know of anyone who might have a grudge against Searle?'

'No one in Salcott. I don't know anything of his friends or enemies elsewhere.'

'Have you any objection to my looking through Searle's belongings?'

'I haven't, but Searle might. What do you expect to find, Inspector?'

'Nothing specific. A man's belongings are very revealing, I find. I am merely looking for suggestion of some sort; help of any kind in a very puzzling situation.'

'I'll take you up now, then—unless there is anything else you want to ask me.'

'No, thank you. You have been very helpful. I wish you could have trusted me far enough to tell me what the quarrel was about——'

'There was no quarrel!' Whitmore said sharply.

'I beg your pardon. I mean, in what way Searle riled you. It would tell me even more about Searle than it would about you; but perhaps it is too much to expect you to see that.'

Whitmore stood by the door, considering this. 'No,' he said slowly. 'No, I do see what you mean. But to tell you involves—— No, I don't think I can tell you.'

'I see you can't. Let us go up.'

As they emerged into the baronial hall from the library where the interview had taken place, Liz had just come out of the drawing-room and was crossing to the stairs. When she saw Grant she paused and her face lighted with joy.'

'Oh!' she said, 'you've come with news of him!'

When Grant said no, that he had no news, she looked puzzled.

'But it was you who introduced him,' she insisted. 'At that party.'

This was news to Walter and Grant could feel his surprise. He could also feel his resentment at that flash of overwhelming joy on Liz's face.

'This, Liz dear,' he said in a cool, faintly malicious tone, 'is Detective Inspector Grant from Scotland Yard.'

'From the Yard! But—you *were* at that party!'

'It is not unheard of for policemen to be interested in the arts,' Grant said, amused. 'But——'

'Oh, please! I didn't mean it that way.'

'I had only looked in at the party to pick up a friend. Searle was standing by the door looking lost because he didn't know Miss Fitch by sight. So I took him over and introduced them. That is all.'

'And now you've come down here to—to investigate—'

'To investigate his disappearance. Have you any theories, Miss Garrowby?'

'I? No. Not even a rudimentary one. It just doesn't make sense. It's *fantastically* senseless.'

'If it isn't too late may I talk to you for a little when I have been through Searle's belongings?'

'No, of course it isn't too late. It isn't ten o'clock yet.' She sounded weary. 'Since this happened time stretches out and out. It's like having—hashish, is it? Are you looking for anything in particular, Inspector.'

'Yes,' Grant said. 'Inspiration. But I doubt if I shall find it.'

'I shall be in the library when you come down. I hope you will find something that will help. It is very dreadful being suspended from a spider's thread this way.'

As he went through Searle's belongings Grant thought about Liz Garrowby—Marta's 'dear nice Liz'—and her relations with William's 'push-ee'. There was never any saying what a woman saw in any man, and Whitmore was of course a celebrity as well as a potentially good husband. He had said as much to Marta, coming away from the party that day. But how right had Marta been about Searle's power to upset? How much had Liz Garrowby felt Searle's charm? How much of that eager welcome of hers in the hall had been joy at Searle's imagined safety and how much mere relief from the burden of suspicion and gloom?

His hands turned over Searle's things with automatic efficiency, but his mind was busy deciding how much or how little to ask Liz Garrowby when he went downstairs again.

Searle had occupied a first-floor room in the battlemented tower that stuck out to the left of the Tudor front door, so that it had windows on three sides of it. It was large and high, and was furnished in very superior Tottenham Court Road, a little too gay and coy for its Victorian amplitude. It was an impersonal room and Searle had evidently done nothing to stamp it with his personality. This struck Grant as odd. He had rarely seen a room, occupied for so long, so devoid of atmosphere. There were brushes on the table, and books by the bedside, but of their owner there was no trace. It might have been a room in a shop window.

Of course it had been swept and tidied since last it was occupied six days ago. But still. But still.

The feeling was so strong that Grant paused to look round and consider. He thought of all the rooms he had searched in his time. They had all—even the hotel rooms—been redolent of their late occupier. But here was nothing but emptiness. An impersonal blank. Searle had kept his personality to himself.

Grant noticed, as Liz had noticed on that first day, how expensive his clothes and luggage were. As he turned over the handkerchiefs in the top drawer he noticed that they had no laundry mark, and wondered a little. Done at home, perhaps. The shirts and linen were marked but the mark was old and probably American.

As well as the two leather suitcases, there was a japanned tin case like a very large paint-box, with the name 'L. Searle' in white letters on the lid. It was fitted with a lock but was unfastened and Grant lifted the lid with some curiosity, only to find that it was filled with Searle's photographic material. It was built on the lines of a paint-box, with a top tray that was made to lift out. Grant hooked out the top tray with his forefingers and surveyed the deeper compartment below it. The lower compartment was full except for an oblong of empty space where something had been taken out. Grant put down the tray he was holding and went to unroll the camp outfit that had been brought back from the river-bank. He wanted to know what fitted into that oblong space.

But there was nothing that fitted.

There were two small cameras in the pack and some rolls of film. Neither separately nor together did they fit into the space in the tin box. Nor did anything else in the pack.

Grant came back and stood for some time considering that empty space. Something roughly 10 inches by 3½ by 4 had been taken out. And it had been taken out when the box was in its present position. Any heaving about of the box would have dislodged the other objects from their packed position and obliterated the empty space.

He would have to ask about that when he went downstairs.

Meanwhile, having given the room a quick going-over, he now went over it in detail. Even so, he nearly missed the vital thing. He had run through the rather untidy handkerchief-and-ties drawer and was in the act of closing it, when something among the ties caught his attention and he picked it out.

It was a woman's glove. A very small woman's glove. A glove about Liz Garrowby's size.

Grant looked for its mate but there was none. It was the usual lover's trophy.

So the beautiful young man had been sufficiently attracted to steal one of his beloved's gloves. Grant found it oddly endearing. An almost Victorian gesture. Nowadays fetish-worship took much more sinister forms.

Well, whatever the glove proved, it surely proved that Searle had meant to come back. One does not leave stolen love-objects in one's tie-drawer to be exposed to the unsympathetic gaze of the stranger.

The question to be decided was: whose glove, and how much or how little did it mean?

Grant put it in his pocket and went downstairs. Liz was waiting for him in the library as she had promised, but he noticed that she had had company. No one person could have smoked so many cigarettes as the ends in the ash-tray indicated. Grant deduced that Walter Whitmore had been in consultation with her over this affair of police interrogation.

But Liz had not forgotten that she was also a secretary and official receptionist for Trimmings, and she had caused drinks to be brought. Grant refused them because he was on duty, but approved of her effort on his behalf.

'I suppose this is only a beginning,' Liz said, indicating the *Wickham Times* (once weekly every Friday) which was lying open on the table. YOUNG MAN MISSING, said a modest headline in an inconspicuous position. And

Walter was referred to as Mr Walter Whitmore, of Trimmings, Salcott St Mary, the well-known commentator.

'Yes,' Grant said. 'The daily Press will have it tomorrow.'

WHITMORE'S COMPANION DROWNED, they would say tomorrow, on the front page. WHITMORE MYSTERY. FRIEND OF WHITMORE DISAPPEARS.

'It is going to be very bad for Walter.'

'Yes. Publicity is suffering from a sort of inflation. Its power is out of all proportion to its worth.'

'What do you think happened to him, Inspector? To Leslie?'

'Well, for a time I had a theory that he might have disappeared of his own accord.'

'Voluntarily! But *why*?'

'That I wouldn't know without knowing more about Leslie Searle. You don't think, for instance, that he was the type to play a practical joke?'

'Oh, *no*. Quite definitely not. He wasn't that kind at all. He was very quiet and—and had excellent taste. He wouldn't see anything funny in practical joking. besides, where could he disappear to with all his belongings left behind? He would have only what he stood up in.'

'About those belongings. Did you ever happen to see inside the japanned tin box that belongs to him?'

'The photographic box. I think I must have once. Because I remember thinking how neatly packed everything was.'

'Something has been taken out of the lower compartment, and I can't find anything that fits the space. Would you be able to tell what is missing, do you think?'

'I'm sure I shouldn't. I don't remember anything in detail. Only the neatness. It was chemical stuff, and slides, and things like that.'

'Did he keep it locked?'

'It *did* lock, I know. Some of the stuff was poisonous. But I don't think it was kept permanently locked. Is it locked now?'

'No. Otherwise I shouldn't have known about the empty space.'

'I thought policemen could open anything.'

'They *can*, but they *may* not.'

She smiled a little and said: 'I was always in trouble with that at school.'

'By the way,' he said, 'do you recognise this glove?' And produced it from his pocket.

'Yes,' she said, mildly interested. 'It looks like one of mine. Where did you find it?'

'In Searle's handkerchief drawer.'

It was exactly like touching a snail, he thought. The instant closing-up and withdrawal. One moment she was frank and unselfconscious. The next moment she was startled and defensive.

'How odd,' she said, through a tight throat. 'He must have picked it up and meant to give it back to me. I keep a spare pair in the pocket of the car, a respectable pair, and drive in old ones. Perhaps one of my respectable pair dropped out one day.'

'I see.'

'That one, certainly, is one of the kind I keep in the car pocket. Presentable enough to go calling or shopping with but not too grand for everyday wear.'

'Do you mind if I keep it for a little?'

'No, of course not. Is it an "exhibit"?' It was a gallant effort to sound light.

'Not exactly. But anything that was in Searle's room is of potential value at the moment.'

'I think that glove is more likely to mislead you than help you, Inspector. But keep it by all means.'

He liked the touch of spirit, and was glad of her quick recovery. He had never enjoyed teasing snails.

'Would Mr Whitmore be able to tell what is missing from that case?'

'I doubt it, but we can see.' She made for the door to summon Walter.

'Or anyone else in the household?'

'Well, Aunt Lavinia wouldn't. She never knows even what is in her own drawers. And Mother wouldn't, because she never goes near the tower room except to put her head in to see that the bed had been done and the place dusted. But we can ask the staff.'

Grant took them up to the tower bedroom and showed them what he meant about the empty space. What had lain in that oblong gap?

'Some chemical that he has already used up?' Walter suggested.

'I thought of that, but all the necessary chemicals are still there and hardly used at all. You can't think of anything that you have seen him with that would fill that gap?'

They could not; and neither could Alice the housemaid. No one did Mr Searle's room but her, she said. A Mrs Clamp came from the village every day to help, but she did not do bedrooms. Just stairs and corridors and offices and that.

Grant watched their faces and speculated. Whitmore was poker-faced; Liz half interested by the puzzle, half troubled; Alice apprehensive that she might be held responsible for whatever was missing from the case.

He was getting nowhere.

Whitmore came to the front door with him, and peering into the dark said: 'Where is your car?'

'I left it down the avenue,' Grant said. 'Goodnight, and thank you for being so helpful.'

He moved away into the darkness and waited while Walter closed the door. Then he walked round the house to the garage. It was still open, and it held three cars. He tried the pockets of all three, but none of them held an odd glove. None of them held any gloves whatever.

IO

WILLIAMS was sitting in the corner of the coffee-room at
the White Hart, consuming a late supper; and the
landlord greeted Grant and went away to bring supper
for him too. Williams, with the aid of the local police,
had spent a long, tiring, and unproductive afternoon
and evening on Grant's theory that Searle might have,
for reasons of his own, disappeared. At ten o'clock,
having interviewed his twenty-third bus conductor, and
the last available railway porter, he had called it a day,
and was now relaxed over beer and sausage-and-mashed.

'Not a thing,' he said, in answer to Grant's question.
'No one even remotely like him. Any luck with you, sir?'

'Nothing that makes the situation any clearer.'

'No letters among his belongings?'

'Not one. They must be all in his wallet, if he has any
at all. Nothing but packets of photographs.'

'Photographs?' Williams's ears pricked.

'Local ones that he has taken since he came here.'

'Oh. Any of Walter Whitmore's girl, by any chance?'

'A very great number indeed.'

'Yes? Posed ones?'

'No, Williams, no. Romantic. Her head against a
sunlit sky with a spray of almond blossom across it.
That kind of thing.'

'Is she photogenic, would you say? A blonde?' ·

'No, she is a small, dark, plainish creature with a nice face.'

'Oh. What does he want to go on photographing her for? Must be in love with her.'

'I wonder,' Grant said; and was silent while food was put in front of him.

'You really ought, just for once, to try those pickles, sir,' Williams said. 'They're wonderful.'

'For the five hundred and seventh time, I do *not* eat pickles. I have a palate, Williams. A precious possession. And I have no intention of prostituting it to pickles. There was something among Searle's things that was a great deal more suggestive than any photograph.'

'What, sir?'

'One of the girl's gloves,' Grant said; and told him where it had been found.

'Well, well,' Williams said, and chewed the information over in silence for a little. 'Doesn't sound as if it had gone very far.'

'What?'

'The affair. If he was still at the stage of stealing her glove. Honestly, sir, in this day and age I didn't imagine that anyone was driven to making do with a glove.'

Grant laughed. 'I told you. She is a nice girl. Tell me, Williams, what kind of object would fit a space 10 inches by 3½ by 4?'

'A bar of soap,' said Williams without hesitation.

'Unlikely. What else?'

'Box of cigarettes?'

'No. Not a smoker.'

'Food of some kind? Processed cheese is that shape.'

'No.'

'Revolver? Revolver in a case, I mean.'

'I wonder. Why should he have a revolver?'

'What space are you trying to fill, sir?' Williams asked, and Grant described the photographic box, and the gap in the neatly fitted compartment.

'Whatever had been there was something solid, so that the outline was hard and clear. Nothing that was still available among his belongings fitted the gap. So either he took it out and got rid of it, or it was removed for some reason after he had disappeared.'

'That would mean that someone at Trimmings is suppressing evidence. You still think Whitmore not the type, sir?'

'Type?'

'Not the bumping-off type.'

'I think Whitmore would be more liable to get into a pet than to see red.'

'But he wouldn't need to see red to drown Searle. A shove when he was in a pet would have done.it, and he mightn't have been able to do anything about rescue in the dark. Then he might lose his head and pretend he knew nothing about it. Heaven knows that happens often enough.'

'You think Whitmore did it but did it in half-accident?'

'I don't know who did it. But it's my firm conviction that Searle is still in the river, sir.'

'But Inspector Rodgers says he dragged it thoroughly.'

'The sergeant in charge at Wickham Police Station says the mud in the bed of the Rushmere goes half-way to Australia.'

'Yes. I know. The Chief Constable, I understand, made the same observation in a less vivid phrase.'

'After all,' Williams said not listening, 'what *could* have become of him if he didn't drown? If all reports are true he wasn't a type you look at and never remember.'

No. That was true. Grant thought of the young man who had stood in Cormac Ross's doorway, and reflected how little the official description of the missing man conveyed the individual they were looking for.

A man, in his early twenties, five feet eight-and-a-half or nine inches, slim build, very fair, grey eyes, straight nose, cheek bones rather high, wide mouth; hatless; wearing belted mackintosh over grey tweed jacket, grey pullover, blue sports shirt, and grey flannels, brown American shoes with instep buckle instead of lacing; low voice with American accent.

No one reading that description would visualise the actuality that was Leslie Searle. On the other hand, as Williams pointed out, no one could set eyes on the actual Searle and not look back for a second glance. No one would see him and not remember.

'Besides, what could he want to disappear *for*?' persisted Williams.

'That I can't guess without knowing much more of his background. I must get the Yard on to it first thing tomorrow. There's a female cousin somewhere in England, but it is his American background that I want to know about. I can't help feeling that the bumping-off trade is more native to California than it is to the B.B.C.'

'No one from California took whatever it was from Searle's case,' Williams pointed out.

'No,' Grant said, contemplative; and went over the

inhabitants of Trimmings in his mind. Tomorrow he would have to begin the collection of alibis. Williams was of course right. It was unlikely to the point of fantasy that Searle should have disappeared in such a manner of his own accord. He had suggested to Liz Garrowby that Searle might have planned a practical joke for Walter's discomfiture, and Liz had scorned the suggestion. But even if Liz had been wrong in her estimate, how could Searle have done it?

'There is still your passing motorist,' he said aloud.

'What's that, sir?'

'We have interviewed the people on the regular transport services, but we have had no way yet of reaching the casual motorist who might have given him a lift.'

Williams, dilated with sausage and beer, smiled benevolently on him. 'You make the Fifty-seventh look like a girl's school, sir.'

'The Fifty-seventh?'

'You die awfully hard. You still in love with that theory about his ducking of his own accord?'

'I still think that he could have walked on from the river bend, up across the fields, to the main Wickham-Crome road and got a lift there. I'll ask Bryce in the morning if we could have a radio S.O.S. about it.'

'And after he got the lift, sir? What then? All his luggage is at Trimmings.'

'We don't know that. We don't know anything about him before he walked into that party of Ross's. He is a photographer; that is all we know for certain. He says he has only a female cousin in England but he may have half a dozen homes and a dozen wives for all we know.'

'Maybe, but why not go in a natural fashion when this trip was finished? After all, he would want to collect on that book they were doing, surely? Why all the mumbo-jumbo?'

'To make things awkward for Walter, perhaps.'

'Yes? You think that? Why?'

'Perhaps because I wouldn't mind making things awkward for Walter myself,' Grant said with a half smile. 'Perhaps after all it is just wishful-thinking on my part.'

'It certainly is going to be very uncomfortable for Whitmore,' Williams said, without any noticeable regret.

'Very. Shouldn't wonder if it leads to civil war.'

'War?'

'The Faithful Whitmorites versus the Doubters.'

'Is he taking it hard?'

'I don't think he quite realises yet what has hit him. He won't, I think, until he sees the daily Press tomorrow morning.'

'Haven't the Press been at him already?'

'They haven't had time. The *Clarion* arrived on the doorstep at five this afternoon, I understand, and went away to get information at the Swan when he failed to get it at Trimmings.'

'Trust the *Clarion* to be first. Whitmore would have done better to see whoever it was. Why didn't he?'

'Waiting for his lawyer to arrive from town, so he said.'

'Who was it, do you know? The *Clarion*.'

'Jammy Hopkins.'

'Jammy! I'd as soon have a flame-thrower on my tail as Jammy Hopkins. He has no conscience whatever. He'll make up a story out of whole cloth if he doesn't get an interview. You know, I begin to be sorry for Walter Whitmore. He couldn't really have given a thought to Jammy, or he wouldn't have been so quick to shove Searle into the river.'

'And who is being Die-Hard now?' Grant said.

II

In the morning Grant telephoned to his chief, but he had no sooner begun his story than Bryce interrupted him.

'That you, Grant? You send back that Man Friday of yours straight away. Benny Skoll cleaned out Poppy Plumtre's bedroom safe last night.'

'I thought all Poppy's valuables were with Uncle.'

'Not since she got herself a new daddy.'

'Are you sure that it's Benny?'

'Quite sure. It has all his trade-marks. The telephone call to get the hall porter out of the way, the lack of finger-prints, the bread-and-jam and milk meal, the exit by the service entrance. Short of signing his name in the visitors' book, he couldn't have written his signature more clearly over it.'

'Ah, well; the day criminals learn to vary their technique we go out of business.'

'I need Williams to pick up Benny. Williams knows Benny like a book. So send him back. How are you doing?'

'Not too well.'

'No? How?'

'We have no corpse. So we have two possibilities: Searle is dead, either by accident or by design; or he has just disappeared for ends of his own.'

'What sort of ends?'

'Practical joke, perhaps.'

'He had better not try that stuff with us.'

'It might, of course, be plain amnesia.'

'It had better be.'

'There are two things I need, sir. A radio S.O.S. is one. And the other is some information from the San Francisco police about Searle. We are working in the dark, knowing nothing about him. His only relation in England is a cousin; a woman artist, with whom he had no contact. Or says he hadn't. She will probably get in touch with us when she sees the papers this morning. But she will probably know very little about him.'

'And you think the San Francisco police will know more?'

'Well, San Francisco was his headquarters, I understand, when he spent the winter months on the Coast, and they can no doubt dig up something about him there. Let us know whether he ever was in any bother and if anyone was liable to kill him for any reason.'

'A lot of people would like to kill a photographer, I should think. Yes, we'll do that.'

'Thank you, sir. And about the S.O.S.?'

'The B.B.C. don't like their nice little radio cluttered up with police messages. What did you want to say?'

'I want to ask anyone who gave a lift to a young man between Wickham and Crome on Wednesday night to get in touch with us.'

'Yes, I'll see to that. I suppose you have covered all the regular services?'

'Everything, sir. Not a sign of him anywhere. And he is hardly inconspicuous. Short of his having a rendezvous with a waiting plane—which only happens in boys' stories, as far as I'm aware—the only way he could have got away from the district is by walking over the fields and getting a lift on the main road.'

'No evidence of homicide?'

'None so far. But I shall see what alibis the locals have, this morning.'

'You push Williams off before you do anything else. I'll send the San Francisco information to the Wickham Station when it comes through.'

'Very good, sir. Thank you.'

Grant hung up and went to tell Williams.

'Damn Benny,' Williams said. 'Just when I was beginning to like this bit of country. It's no day to wrestle with Benny anyhow.'

'Is he tough?'

'Benny? No! He's a horror. He'll cry and carry on and say that we are hounding him, and that he is no sooner out of stir and trying to make good—"make good"! Benny!—than we are down on him to come and be questioned, and what chance has he in the circs. and so on. He turns my stomach. If Benny saw an honest day's work coming his way he'd run for his life. He's a wonderful cryer, though. He once got a question asked in Parliament. You'd wonder how some of those M.P.s ever had brains enough to ask for a railway ticket from their home towns. Have I got to take a *train* to town?'

'I expect Rodgers will give you a car to Crome and you can get a fast train there,' Grant said, smiling at the horror on his colleague's face at the thought of train travel. He himself went back to the telephone and called Marta Hallard at the Mill House in Salcott St Mary.

'Alan!' she said. 'How nice. Where are you?'

'At the White Hart in Wickham.'

'You poor dear!'

'Oh, it isn't too bad.'

'Don't be so noble. You know it is primitive to the point of being penitential. Have you heard about our latest sensation, by the way?'

'I have. That is why I am in Wickham.'

There was a complete silence at that.

Then Marta said: 'You mean the *Yard* are interested in Leslie Searle's drowning?'

'In Searle's disappearance, let us say.'

'You mean, that there is some truth in this rumour of a quarrel with Walter?'

'I'm afraid I can't discuss it over the telephone. What I wanted to ask you was whether you would be at home this evening if I came along.'

'But you must come and stay, of course. You can't stay at that dreary place. I'll tell Mrs ——'

'Thank you with all my heart, but I can't do that. I must be here in Wickham at the centre of things. But if you like to give me dinner ——'

'Of course I shall give you dinner. You shall have a beautiful meal, my dear. With one of my omelets and one of Mrs Thrupp's chickens, and a bottle from the cellar that will take the taste of the White Hart beer out of your mouth.'

So, a little heartened at the prospect of civilisation at the end of the day, Grant went out on his day's task, and he began with Trimmings. If there was to be a reckoning of alibis it was fitting that the inhabitants of Trimmings should be the first to give an account of themselves.

It was a fine blue morning, growing soft after an early

frost, and no day, as Williams had pointed out, to waste on the Bennys of this life; but the sight of Trimmings standing up unblushingly in the bright sunlight restored Grant's wavering good humour. Last night it had been a lighted doorway in the dark. Today it stood revealed, extravagantly monstrous, in all its smug detail, and Grant was so enraptured that his foot came down on the brake and he brought the car to a standstill at the curve of the drive, and sat there gazing.

'I know just how you are feeling,' a voice said at his elbow. And there was Liz; a little heavy-eyed, he noticed, but otherwise calm and friendly.

'Good morning,' he said. 'I was a little dashed this morning because I couldn't drop everything and go fishing. But I feel better now.'

'It is a beauty, isn't it,' she agreed. 'You don't quite believe it is there at all. You feel that no one could possibly have thought it up; it just appeared.'

Her thoughts shifted from the house to his presence, and he saw the question coming.

'I am sorry to be a nuisance, but I am busy this morning getting rid of the undergrowth in this case.'

'Undergrowth?'

'I want to get rid of all the people who can't possibly enter into the case at all.'

'I see. You are collecting alibis.'

'Yes.' He opened the car door, so that she might ride the short distance to the house.

'Well, I hope we have good ones. I regret to say that I haven't one at all. It was the first thing I thought of when I knew who you were. It's very odd, isn't it, how guilty an innocent person feels when he can't account for himself on the umpteenth inst. Do you want everyone's alibi? Aunt Lavinia's and mother's and all?'

'And those of the staff, too. Of everyone who had any connection with Leslie Searle.'

'Well, you had better start with Aunt Vin. Before she begins her morning chore. She dictates for two hours every morning, and she likes to begin punctually.'

'Where were you, Miss Garrowby?' he asked as they arrived at the door.

'At the material time?' He thought she was being deliberately cold-blooded about it; the 'material time' was when Leslie Searle had presumably lost his life, and he did not think that she was forgetting that fact.

'Yes. On Wednesday night.'

'I had what they call in detective stories "retired to my room". And don't tell me that it was "early to retire", either. I know it was. I like going upstairs early. I like being alone at the end of the day.'

'Do you read?'

'Don't tell, Inspector, but I write.'

'You too?'

'Do I disappoint you?'

'You interest me. What do you write—or shouldn't I ask?'

'I write innocuous heroines out of my system, that's all.'

'Tilda the tweeny with the hare-lip and the homicidal tendencies, as antidote to Maureen.'

She looked at him for a long moment and then said: 'You are a very odd sort of policeman.'

'I suspect that it is your idea of policemen that is odd,' Grant said briskly. 'Will you tell your aunt that I am here?'

But there was no need to announce him. Miss Fitch was in the hall as Liz ran up the steps, and she said in tones more surprised than grieved:

'Liz, you are five minutes late!' Then she saw the Inspector, and said: 'Well, well, they were right. They said that no one would ever take you for a policeman. Come in, Inspector. I have wanted so much to meet you. Officially, as it were. Our last encounter could hardly be termed a meeting, could it. Come into the morning-room. That is where I work.'

Grant apologised for keeping her from her morning's dictation, but she professed herself glad to postpone for at least ten minutes her business with 'the tiresome girl'. Grant took the 'tiresome girl' to be the current Fitch heroine.

Miss Fitch, too, it seemed, had retired early on Wednesday night. At half-past nine, to be exact.

'When a family are in each other's pocket all day long, as we are,' she said, 'they tend to go to their rooms early at night.' She had watched a radio play, and had lain awake a little, half-listening for her sister coming in, but had fallen asleep quite early after all.

'Coming in?' Grant said. 'Was Mrs Garrowby out, then?'

'Yes. She was at a W.R.I. meeting.'

He asked her about Searle, then. What she had thought of him, and what in her opinion he was liable to do or not to do. She was surprisingly guarded about Searle, he thought; as if she were picking her steps; and he wondered why.

When he said: 'Did Searle, in your opinion, show signs of being in love with your niece?' she looked startled, and said 'No, of course not!' too quickly and too emphatically.

'He did not pay her attentions?'

'My dear man,' Miss Fitch said, '*any* American pays a girl attentions. It is a conditioned reflex. As automatic as breathing.'

'You think he was not seriously interested in her?'

'I am sure that he wasn't.'

'Your nephew told me last night that he and Searle had telephoned to you each night on their way down the river.'

'Yes.'

'Did everyone in the household know about the message on Wednesday night? I mean, know where the two men were camped?'

'I expect so. The family certainly did; and the staff were always anxious to hear about their progress so I suppose everyone knew.'

'Thank you very much, Miss Fitch. You have been very kind.'

She called Liz in, and Liz took him to her mother and went back to the morning-room to record the doings of the latest Maureen.

Mrs Garrowby was another person without an alibi. She had been at the W.R.I. meeting at the village hall, had left there when the meeting broke up at half-past nine, had accompanied Miss Easton-Dixon part of the way home and had left her where their roads branched. She had come in about ten; or later, perhaps: she had strolled home because it was a lovely night; and had locked up the front of the house. The back door was always locked by Mrs Brett, the cook-housekeeper.

Emma Garrowby did not fool Grant for a moment. He had met her counterpart too often; that ruthless maternalism masquerading in a placid exterior. Had Searle got in the way of plans she had made for her daughter?

He asked her about Searle, and there was no step-picking at all. He had been a charming young man, she said. Quite exceptionally charming. They all liked him enormously, and were shattered by this tragedy.

Grant caught himself receiving this mentally with an expressive monosyllable.

He felt a little suffocated by Mrs Garrowby, and was glad when she went away to find Alice for him.

Alice had been walked-out on Wednesday night by the under-gardener, and had come in at a quarter past ten, whereupon the door had been locked behind her by Mrs Brett, and they had gone up together, after having a cup of cocoa, to their rooms in the back wing. Alice really was shattered by the fate that had overtaken Leslie Searle. Never, she said, had she had to do for a nicer young man. She had met dozens of young men, gentlemen *and* others, who considered a girl's ankles, but Mr Searle was the only one who considered a girl's feet.

'*Feet?*'

She had said as much to Mrs Brett, and to Edith, the parlourmaid. He would say: 'You can do this or that, and that will save you coming up again, won't it.' And she could only conclude that this was an American characteristic, because no Englishman she had ever come across had ever cared two hoots whether you had to come up again or not.

Edith, too, it seemed, mourned for Leslie Searle; not because he considered her feet but because he was so good-looking. Edith proved to be very superior and refaynod. Much too refayned to be walked out by an under-gardener. She had gone to her room to watch the same play that her mistress was watching. She heard Mrs Brett and Alice come up to bed, but the wing bedrooms were too far away to hear anyone come into the main block, so she did not know when Mrs Garrowby had come in.

Neither did Mrs Brett. After dinner, Mrs Brett said, the family did not worry the staff at all. Edith laid out the bed-time drinks, and after that the baize door in the hall was not normally opened again until the following morning. Mrs Brett had been nine years with Miss Fitch, and Miss Fitch could trust her to manage the staff and the staff premises.

When Grant went to the front door on his way to the car he found Walter Whitmore propped against the terrace wall. He bade Grant good morning and hoped that the alibis had been satisfactory.

It seemed to Grant that Walter Whitmore was visibly deteriorating. Even the few hours since last night had made a difference. He wondered how much a reading of this morning's papers had contributed to the slackening of Walter's facial structure.

'Have the Press been hounding you yet?' he asked.

'They were here just after breakfast.'

'Did you talk to them?'

'I saw them, if that is what you mean. There wasn't much I could say. They'll get far more copy down at the Swan.'

'Did your lawyer come?'

'Yes. He's asleep.'

'Asleep!'

'He left London at half-past five, and saw me through the interview. He had to leave things in a hurry so he didn't get to bed last night till two this morning. If you take my meaning.'

Grant left him with an illogical feeling of relief and went down to the Swan. He ran his car into the paved brick yard at the rear of it and knocked at the side door.

A bolt was drawn with noisy impatience, and Reeve's face appeared in the gap. 'It's not a bit of use,' he said. 'You'll have to wait till opening time.'

'As a policeman, I appreciate that snub at its true value,' Grant said. 'But I'd like to come in and talk to you for a moment.'

'You look more Service than Police, if you ask me,' said the ex-Marine, amused, as he led the way into the bar parlour. 'You're the spit of a Major we had with us Up The Straights once. Vandaleur was his name. Ever come across him?'

Grant had not come across Major Vandaleur.

'Well, what can I do for you, sir? It's about this Searle affair, I take it.'

'Yes. You can do two things for me. I want your considered opinion—and I mean considered—on the relations between Whitmore and Searle on Wednesday evening. And I should like a list of all the people in the bar that night and the times they left.'

Reeve had all a service man's objective attitude to a happening. He had no desire to dress it up, or to make it reflect his own personality as an artist did. Grant felt himself relaxing. It was almost like listening to the report of one of his own men. There was no obvious ill-feeling between the men, Reeve said. He would not have noticed them at all, if they had not been isolated by the fact that no one moved away from the bar to join them. Normally, someone or other would have moved over to resume a conversation that had begun when they were at the bar together. But on Wednesday there was something in their unconsciousness of the rest that kept people from intruding.

'They were like two dogs walking round each other,' Reeve said. 'No row, but a sort of atmosphere. The row might burst out any minute, if you see what I mean.'

'Did you see Whitmore go?'

'No one did. The boys were having an argument about who played cricket for Australia in what year. They paused when the door banged, that was all. Then Bill Maddox, seeing that Searle was alone, went over and talked to him. Maddox keeps the garage at the end of the village.'

'Thanks. And now the list of those in the bar.'

Grant wrote the list down; county names, most of them, unchanged since Domesday Book. As he went out to get his car he said: 'Have you any Press staying in the house?'

'Three,' Reeve said. 'The *Clarion*, the *Morning News*, and the *Post*. They're all out now, sucking the village dry.'

'Also ran: Scotland Yard,' Grant said wryly, and drove away to see Bill Maddox.

At the end of the village was a high clapboarded structure on which faded paint said: WILLIAM MADDOX

AND SON, CARPENTERS AND BOATBUILDERS. At one corner of this building a bright black and yellow sign pointed into the yard at the side and said simply: GARAGE.

'You manage to make the best of both worlds, I see,' he said to Bill Maddox when he had introduced himself, and tilted his head at the sign.

'Oh, MADDOX AND SON is Father, not me.'

'I thought that perhaps you were "SON".'

Bill looked amused. 'Oh, no; my *grandfather* was SON. That's my greatgrandfather's business. And still the best woodworkers this side of the county, though it's me that says it. You looking for information, Inspector?'

Grant got all the information Maddox could give him, and as he was going away Maddox said: 'You happen to know a newspaper-man called Hopkins, by any chance?'

'Hopkins of the *Clarion*? We have met.'

'He was round here for hours this morning, and do you know what that bloke actually believes? He believes that the whole thing is just a publicity stunt to sell that book they planned to write.'

The combination of this typically Hopkins reaction and Bill's bewildered face was too much for Grant. He leant against the car and laughed.

'It's a debasing life, a journalist's,' he said. 'And Jammy Hopkins is a born debase-ee, as a friend of mine would say.'

'Oh,' said Bill, still puzzled. 'Silly, I call it. Plain silly.'

'Do you know where I can find Serge Ratoff, by the way?'

'I don't suppose he's out of bed yet, but if he is you'll find him propping up the counter of the post-office.

The post-office is in the shop. Half-way up the street. Serge lives in the lean-to place next door to it.'

But Serge had not yet reached his daily stance by the post-office counter. He was coming down the street from the newsagent's with a paper under his arm. Grant had never seen him before, but he knew the occupational signs well enough to spot a dancer in a village street. The limp clothes covering an apparently weedy body, the general air of undernourishment, the wilting appearance that made one feel that the muscles must be flabby as tired elastic. It was a never-ceasing amazement to Grant that the flashing creatures who tossed ballerinas about with no more effort than a slight gritting of teeth, went out of the stage door looking like under-privileged barrow boys.

He brought the car to a halt at the pavement as he came level with Serge, and greeted him.

'Mr Ratoff?'

'That is me.'

'I'm Detective-Inspector Grant. May I speak to you for a moment?'

'Everyone speaks to me,' Serge said complacently. 'Why not you?'

'It is about Leslie Searle.'

'Ah, yes. He has become drowned. Delightful.'

Grant offered some phrases on the virtue of discretion.

'Ah, *discretion*!' said Serge, making five syllables of it. 'A bourgeois quality.'

'I understand that you had a quarrel with Searle.'

'Nothing of the sort.'

'But——'

'I fling a mug of beer in his face, that is all.'

'And you don't call that a quarrel?'

'Of *course* not. To quarrel is to be on a level, equal, how do you say, of the same rank. One does not quarrel with *canaille*. My grandfather in Russia would have taken a whip to him. This is England and decadent, and so I fling beer over him. It is a gesture, at least.'

When Grant recounted this conversation to Marta, she said: 'I can't think what Serge would do without that grandfather in Russia. His father left Russia when he was three—Serge can't speak a word of Russian and he is half Neapolitan anyhow—but all his fantasies are built on that grandfather in Russia.'

'You will understand,' Grant said patiently, 'that it is necessary for the police to ask all those who knew Searle for an account of their movements on Wednesday night.'

'Is it? How tiresome for you. It is a sad life, a policeman's. The movements. So limited, so rudimentary.' Serge made himself into a semaphore, and worked his arms marionette-wise in a travesty of point-duty signals. 'Tiresome. Very tiresome. Lucid, of course, but without subtlety.'

'Where were you on Wednesday night from nine o'clock onwards?' Grant said, deciding that an indirect approach was just a waste of time.

'I was dancing,' Serge said.

'Oh. At the village hall?'

Serge looked as if he were going to faint.

'You suggest that *I*, that I, *Serge Ratoff*, was taking part in a '*op*?'

'Then where were you dancing?'

'By the river.'

'*What?*'

135

'I work out the choreography for a new ballet. I burst with ideas there by the river on a spring night. They rise up in me like fountains. There is so much atmosphere there that I get drunk on it. I can do anything. I work out a very charming idea to go with the river music of Mashako. It begins with a——'

'What part of the river?'

'What?'

'What *part* of the river?'

'How should I know? The atmosphere is the same over all.'

'Well, did you go up river or down, from Salcott?'

'Oh, up, most certainly.'

'Why "most certainly"?'

'I need the wide flat spaces to dance. Up river they are there. Down river from the village it is all steep banks and tiresome root crops. Roots. Clumsy, obscene things. They——'

'Could you identify the place where you were dancing on Wednesday night?'

'Identify?'

'Point it out to me.'

'How can I? I don't even remember where it was.'

'Can you remember if you saw anyone while you were there?'

'No one who was memorable?'

'Memorable?'

'I trip over lovers in the grass now and then, but they— how you say, go with the house. They are part of the— the set-up. Not memorable.'

'Do you remember, then, what time you left the river bank on Wednesday night?'

'Ah, yes, that I remember perfectly.'

'When was it that you left?'

'When the shooting star fell.'

'What time was that?'

'How should I know? I dislike shooting stars. They make butterflies in my stomach. Though I did think that it would be a very fine ending to my ballet to have a shooting star. A *Spectre de la Rose* leap, you know, that would set the town talking, and show them that I can still——'

'Mr Ratoff, can you suggest how Leslie Searle came to be in the river?'

'Came to be? He fell in, I suppose. Such a pity. Pollution. The river is so beautiful it should be kept for beautiful things. Ophelia. Shallott. Do you think Shallott would make a ballet? All the things she sees in the mirror? It is an idea, that, isn't it?'

Grant gave up.

He left his car where it was and walked up the street to where the flat stone front of Hoo House broke the pinks and chromes and limes of the village's plastered gables. The house stood on the pavement like the other cottages, but three steps to the front door raised the ground floor of the house above street level. It withdrew itself a little, in a dignity entirely natural, from everyday affairs. As Grant pulled the Victorian bell in its bright brass circle he spared a thought to bless the man, whoever he was, who had been responsible for restoring the place. He had preserved the structure but had made no attempt to turn it back into its original form and so make a museum piece of it; the tale of the centuries was there, from the worn mounting-block to the brass bell. A great amount of money had obviously been spent to bring it to its present condition of worthiness, and Grant wondered if perhaps the saving of Hoo House was sufficient to justify Toby Tullis's existence.

The door was opened by a manservant who might have walked out of one of Toby's plays. He stood in the doorway, polite but impenetrable; a one-man road-block.

'Mr Tullis does not see anyone before lunch,' he said in answer to Grant's inquiry. 'He works in the morning. The appointment with the Press is for two o'clock.' He began to move his hand towards the door.

'Do I look like Press?' Grant said tartly.

'Well—no, I can't say that you do—sir.'

'Shouldn't you have a little tray?' Grant said, suddenly silky.

The man turned submissively and took a silver card tray from the Jacobean chest in the hall.

Grant dropped a piece of pasteboard on to the tray and said: 'Present my compliments to Mr Tullis and say that I would be grateful for three minutes of his time.'

'Certainly, sir,' said the man, not allowing his eyes to stray even to the vicinity of the card. 'Will you be kind enough to step into the hall and wait.'

He disappeared into a room at the rear of the house, and closed the door behind him on some very unworkmanlike sounds of chatter. But he was back in a moment. Would Inspector Grant come this way, please. Mr Tullis would be very pleased to see him.

The room at the back, Grant found, looked into a large garden sloping down to the river-bank; it was another world altogether from the village street that he had just left. It was a sitting-room, furnished with the most perfect 'pieces' that Grant had ever seen out of a museum. Toby, in a remarkable dressing-gown, was sitting behind an array of silver coffee things; and behind him, in still more remarkable day clothes, hovered a callow and eager young man clutching a notebook. The notebook, from its virgin condition, appeared to be more a badge of office than the implement of a craft.

'You are modest, Inspector!' Toby said, greeting him. 'Modest?'

'Three minutes! Even the Press expect ten.'

It had been meant as a compliment to Grant, but the effect was merely a reminder that Toby was the most-interviewed individual in the English-speaking world and that his time was priceless. As always, what Toby did was a little 'off-key'.

He presented the young man as Giles Verlaine, his secretary, and offered Grant coffee. Grant said that it was at once too late and too early for him, but would Mr Tullis go on with his breakfast; and Toby did.

'I am investigating the disappearance of Leslie Searle,' Grant said. 'And that involves, I'm afraid, some disturbance of people who are only remotely connected with Searle. We have to ask everyone at Salcott who knew Searle to account for their time, as far as they can, on Wednesday night.'

'Inspector, you offer me a felicity I had never hoped to enjoy. I have always been madly desirous of being asked what I was doing at nine-thirty p.m. on the night of Friday the 13th, but I never really dared to hope that it would happen to me.'

'Now that it has happened, I hope your alibi is worthy of the occasion.'

'It has the virtue of simplicity, at least. Giles and I spent the hours of that lovely midnight discussing Act II, Scene 1. Pedestrian, Inspector, but necessary. I am a business man.'

Grant glanced from the business man to Giles, and decided that in his present stage of discipleship the young man would probably confess to the murder if it would pleasure Toby. A little thing like providing an alibi would be merely routine.

'And Mr Verlaine corroborates that, of course,' Grant said.

'Yes, oh yes, of course; of course I do; yes,' said Giles, squandering affirmatives in the service of his patron.

'It is a tragic thing indeed, this drowning,' Toby said, sipping coffee. 'The sum total of the world's beauty is not so great that we can afford to waste any. A Shelleyan end, of course, and to that extent fitting. Do you know the Shelley Memorial at Oxford, Inspector?'

Grant knew the Memorial and it reminded him of an overboiled chicken, but he refrained from saying so. Nor did Toby expect an answer.

'A lovely thing. Drowning is surely the ideal way of going out of this life.'

'After a close acquaintance with a great variety of corpses taken from the water, I can't say that I agree with you.'

Toby cocked a fish-scale eye at him, and said: 'Don't shatter my illusions, Inspector. You are worse than Silas Weekley. Silas is always pointing out the nastiness of life. Have you got Silas's alibi, by the way?'

'Not yet. I understand that he hardly knew Mr Searle.'

'That wouldn't stop Silas. I shouldn't wonder if he did it as a bit of local colour.'

'Local colour?'

'Yes. According to Silas country existence is one cesspool of rape, murder, incest, abortion, and suicide, and perhaps Silas thinks that it is time that Salcott St Mary lived up to his idea of it. Do you read our Silas, Inspector?'

'I'm afraid not.'

'Don't apologise. It's an acquired taste. Even his wife hasn't acquired it yet, if all reports are true. But then, poor woman, she is so busy suckling and suffering that she probably has no time to spare for the consideration of the abstract. No one seems to have indicated to her the possibilities of contraception. Of course, Silas has a "thing" about fertility. He holds that the highest function of a woman is the manufacture of progeny. So disheartening for a woman, don't you feel, to be weighed against a rabbit, and to know that she will inevitably be found wanting. Life, by Fertility out of Ugliness. That is how Silas sees it. He hates beauty. Beauty is an offence. He must mash it down and make it fertile. Make mulch of it. Of course he is just a little crazy, poor sweet, but it is a very profitable kind of craziness, so one need not drench oneself in tears about it. One of the secrets of a successful life is to know how to be a little profitably crazy.'

Grant wondered whether this was merely a normal sample of Toby's chatter, or whether it was designed to edge him on to Silas Weekley. Where a man's personality is entirely façade, as in the case of Toby Tullis, it was difficult to decide how much of the façade was barricade and how much was mere poster-hoarding.

'You didn't see Searle at all on Wednesday evening?' he said.

No, Toby had not seen him. His time for the pub was before dinner, not after.

'I don't want to be intrusive, Inspector, but there seems to me a needless furore over a simple drowning.'

'Why drowning?'

'Why not?'

'We have no evidence at all that Searle was drowned, and some fairly conclusive evidence that he wasn't.'

'That he wasn't? What evidence have you that he wasn't?'

'The river has been dragged for his body.'

'Oh, that!'

'What we are investigating, Mr Tullis, is the disappearance of a man in Salcott St Mary on Wednesday night.'

'You really ought to see the vicar, Inspector. He has the perfect solution for you.'

'And what is that?'

'The dear vicar believes that Searle was never really here at all. He holds that Searle was merely a demon who took human shape for a little, and disappeared when the joke grew stale or the—the juice ran dry, so to speak.'

'Very interesting.'

'I suppose you never saw Searle, Inspector?'

'Oh, yes. I have met him.'

This surprised Toby so much that Grant was amused.

'The demon attended a party in Bloomsbury, just before he came to Salcott,' he said.

'My dear Inspector, you *must* see the vicar. This contribution to the predilections of demons is of inestimable value to research.'

'Why did you ask me if I had ever seen Searle?'

'Because he was so perfectly what one would imagine a materialised demon to be.'

'His good-looks, you mean?'

'Was it only a question of good-looks?' Toby said, half quizzing half in challenge.

'No,' said Grant. 'No.'

'Do you think Searle was a wrong 'un?' Toby said, forgetting the façade for a moment and dropping into the vernacular.

'There is no evidence whatever on that score.'

'Ah, me,' Toby said, resuming the façade with a small mock-sigh. 'The blank wall of bureaucratic caution. I have few ambitions left in life, Inspector, but one of them is a passionate desire to know what made Leslie Searle tick.'

'If I ever find out, bureaucratic caution will crack sufficiently to let you know,' Grant said, getting up to go.

He stood for a moment looking out at the bright garden with the gleam of the river at the far end.

'This might be a country house, miles from anywhere,' he said.

Toby said that that was one of the charms of Hoo House, but that, of course, most of the cottages on the river side of the street had gardens that ran to the river, but most of them were broken into allotments or market gardens of some sort. It was the keeping of the Hoo House grounds as lawns and trees that made it spacious seeming.

'And the river makes a boundary without breaking the view. It is a sadly mixed blessing, the river.'

'Mosquitoes?'

'No; every now and then it has an overwhelming desire to get into the house. About once in every six winters it succeeds. My caretaker woke one morning last winter to find the boat knocking against his bedroom window.'

'You keep a boat?'

'Just as a prop. A punt affair that is pleasant to lie in on summer afternoons.'

Grant thanked him for being so helpful, apologised once more for having intruded on his breakfast, and took his leave. Toby showed signs of wanting to show him the house, but Grant avoided that for three reasons: he had work to do, he had already seen most of the house in the illustrated press, and he had an odd reluctance to be shown the world's finest craftsmanship by a slick little operator like Toby Tullis.

12

SILAS WEEKLEY lived in a cottage down the lane that
led to the far bend of the river. Or rather, that started
off towards the river. The lane, where it met the fields,
turned at right-angles along the back of the village, only
to turn up again and rejoin the village street. It was an
entirely local affair. In the last cottage before the fields
lived Silas Weekley, and Grant, 'proceeding' there
police-fashion, was surprised to find it so poor a dwelling.
It was not only that Weekley was a best-seller and could
therefore afford a home that was more attractive than
this, but there had been no effort to beautify the place;
no generosity of paint and wash such as the other cottagers
had used to make the street of Salcott St Mary a delight
to the eye. No window plants, no trim curtains. The
place had a slum air that was strange in its surroundings.

The cottage door was open and the combined howls of
an infant and a child poured out into the sunny morning.
An enamel basin of dirty water stood in the porch, the
soap bubbles on it bursting one by one in slow resignation:
An animal toy of soft fur, so worn and grubby as to be
unidentifiable as any known species, lay on the floor.
The room beyond was unoccupied for the moment, and
Grant stood observing it in a kind of wonder. It was
poorly furnished and untidy beyond belief.

The crying continued to come from some room in

the rear, so Grant knocked loudly on the front door. At his second knock, a woman's voice called: 'Just leave it there, thank you.' At his third knock supplemented with a call, she came from the darkness at the back and moved forward to inspect him.

'Mrs Weekley?' Grant said doubtfully.

'Yes, I'm Mrs Weekley.'

She must have been pretty once. Pretty and intelligent; and independent. Grant remembered hearing somewhere that Weekley had married an elementary school teacher. She was wearing a sacking apron over a print wrapper, and the kind of old shoes that a woman all too easily gets used to as good enough to do chores in. She had not bothered to put on stockings, and the shoes had left smudges on her bare insteps. Her unwaved hair was pulled back into a tight desperate knot, but the front strands were too short to be confined there for long and now hung down on either side of her face. It was a rather long face and very tired.

Grant said that he would like to see her husband for a moment.

'Oh.' She took it in slowly, as if her mind were still with the crying children. 'I'm sorry things are so untidy,' she said vaguely. 'My girl from the village didn't come today. She often doesn't. It just depends on how she is feeling. And with the children it is difficult——. I don't think I can disturb my husband in the middle of the morning.' Grant wondered whether she considered the children were making no disturbance at all. 'He writes in the morning, you see.'

'I see. But if you would give him my card I think he will see me.'

'Are you from the publishers?'

'No, I'm——'

'Because I think it would be better to wait, and not interrupt him. He could meet you at the Swan, couldn't he? Just before lunch, perhaps.'

'No, I'm afraid that I must see him. You see, it is a matter——'

'It is very important that he shouldn't be disturbed. It interrupts his train of thought, and then he finds it difficult to—to get back. He writes very slowly—carefully, I mean—sometimes only a paragraph a day, so you see it is——'

'Mrs Weekley,' Grant said, bluntly, 'please give that card to your husband and say that I must see him, whatever he happens to be doing.'

She stood with the card in her fingers, not even glancing at it, her mind obviously busy with the search for some excuse that would convince him. And he was all of a sudden aware that she was afraid to take that card to her husband. Afraid to interrupt him.

To help her, he said that surely there would be no interruption where the children had been making so much noise. Her husband could hardly be concentrating very hard.

'Oh, he doesn't work here,' she said. 'In the house, I mean. He has a little house of his own at the end of the garden.'

Grant took back the card she was holding, and said grimly: 'Will you show me the way, Mrs Weekley?'

Dumbly she led him through a dark kitchen where a toddler sat splay-legged on the floor enjoying his tears, and an infant in a perambulator sobbed in elemental fury. Beyond, in the bright sunshine of the garden, a boy of three or so was throwing stones from the pebble path against the wooden door of an outhouse, an unproductive occupation which nevertheless made a satisfying noise.

'Stop that, Freddy,' she said automatically, and Freddy as automatically went on throwing the stones against the door.

The back garden was a long thin strip of ground that ran along the side of the back lane, and at the very end of it, a long way from the house, was a wooden shed. Mrs Weekley pointed it out and said:

'Perhaps you would just go and introduce yourself, would you? The children will be coming in from school for their midday meal and it isn't ready.'

'Children?' Grant said.

'Yes, the three eldest. So if you don't mind.'

'No, of course I don't mind,' Grant said. Indeed, few things would please him like interrupting the great Silas Weekley this morning, but he refrained from saying so to Silas Weekley's wife.

He knocked twice on the door of the wooden hut—a very trim wooden hut—without getting an answer, and so opened the door.

Silas Weekley swung round from the table at which he was writing and said: 'How *dare* you walk into my——' and then stopped as he saw Grant. He had quite obviously expected the intruder to be his wife.

'Who are you?' he said rudely. 'If you are a journalist you will find that rudeness doesn't pay. This is private ground and you are trespassing.'

'I am Detective-Inspector Grant from Scotland Yard,' Grant said and watched the news sink home.

After a moment or two Silas got his lower jaw under control again and said: 'And what do you want, may I ask?' It was an attempt at truculence and it was not convincing.

Grant said his regulation piece about investigating the disappearance of Leslie Searle and accounting for the movements of all those who knew Searle, and noted with the unoccupied half of his mind that the ink on the script that Weekley was working on was not only dry but dark. It was yesterday's ink. Weekley had done not a line this morning although it was now past noon.

At the mention of Searle Weekley began a diatribe against moneyed dilettantes which—in view of Weekley's income and the sum total of his morning's work—Grant thought inappropriate. He cut him short and asked what he had been doing on Wednesday night.

'And if I do not choose to tell you?'

'I record your refusal and go away.'

Weekley did not like the sound of this, so he muttered something about being badgered by the police.

'All that I am doing,' Grant pointed out, 'is asking for your co-operation as a citizen. As I have pointed out, it is within your right to refuse co-operation.'

Silas said sulkily that he had been writing on Wednesday night from supper-time onwards.

'Any witnesses to that?' Grant asked, wasting no frills on Silas.

'My wife, of course.'

'She was here with you?'

'No, of course not. She was in the house.'

'And you were here alone?'

'I was.'

'Thank you and good-morning,' Grant said walking out of the hut and shutting the door crisply behind him.

The morning smelt very fresh and sweet. The sour smell of vomited milk and rough-dried dish-cloths that had hung about the house was nothing to the smell of soured humanity that filled the place where Silas Weekley worked. As he walked back to the house he remembered that it was from this joyless and distorted mind that the current English 'masterpieces' came. The thought did nothing to reassure him. He avoided the joyless house, where the agitated clattering of pans (an appropriate orchestration, he couldn't help thinking) conveyed the preoccupation of its mistress, and walked round the side of it to the front gate, accompanied by Freddy.

'Hullo, Freddy,' he said, sorry for the bored brat.

'Hullo,' Freddy said without enthusiasm.

'Isn't there a more exciting game than flinging stones at a door?'

'No,' said Freddy.

'Couldn't you find one if you looked about you?'

'No,' said Freddy, with cold finality.

Grant stood for a moment contemplating him.

'There will never be any doubt about *your* paternity, Frederick,' he said, and walked away up the lane to the spot where he had left his car.

It was down this lane that Leslie Searle had walked on Wednesday night, calling farewells to the group in the village street. He had walked past the Weekley cottage to where a stile led into the first of the fields that lay between the village and the river bend.

At least that is what one took for granted that he did.

He could have walked along the back lane and come to the village street again. But there would have been little point, surely, in that. He was never seen again in the village. He had walked into the darkness of the lane and disappeared.

A little crazy, Tullis had said of Silas Weekley. But Silas Weekley didn't strike Grant as being crazy. A sadist, perhaps. A megalomaniac almost certainly. A man sick of a twisted vanity. But actually crazy no.

Or would an alienist think differently?

One of the most famous alienists in the country had once said to him that to write a book was to give oneself away. (Someone else had said the same thing more wittily and more succinctly, but he could not think at the moment who it was.) There was unconscious betrayal in every line, said the alienist. What, wondered Grant, would the alienist's verdict be after reading one of Silas Weekley's malignant effusions? That it was the outpouring of a petty mind, a mere fermentation of vanity? Or that it was a confession of madness?

He thought for a moment of going back to the Swan and ringing up Wickham police station from there, but the Swan would be busy just now and the telephone a far from confidential affair. He decided to go back to Wickham and have lunch there, so that he could see Inspector Rodgers at his leisure and pick up any messages that might be waiting for him from Headquarters.

In Wickham he found the higher orders at the police station preparing to retire into the peace of the weekend, and the lower ranks preparing for the weekly liveliness of Saturday night. Rodgers had little to say—he was never a talkative man—and nothing to report. The disappearance of Searle was the talk of Wickham, he said, now that the morning papers had made it general news; but no one had come in to suggest that they had seen him.

'Not even a "nut" to confess to the murder,' he said dryly.

'Well, that is a nice change,' Grant said.

'He'll be along, he'll be along,' Rodgers said resignedly, and invited Grant home to lunch.

But Grant preferred to eat at the White Hart.

He was sitting in the dining-room of the White Hart eating the unpretentious but ample lunch that they provided, when the radio music in the kitchen ceased, and presently, oddly urbane among the castanet racket, came the voice of the announcer.

'Before the news, here is a police message. Would anyone who gave a lift to a young man on Wednesday night on the road between Wickham and Crome, in Orfordshire, or anywhere in that vicinity, please communicate with Scotland Yard——'

'Telephone Whitehall One Two One Two,' chanted the kitchen staff happily.

And then there was a rush of high-pitched conversation as the staff fell to on this latest tit-bit of news.

Grant ate the very good roly-poly without relish and went out again into the sunlight. The streets, which had been teeming with Saturday shoppers when he came in to lunch, were deserted, the shops shut. He drove out of town wishing once more that he was going fishing. How had he ever chosen a profession where he could not count on a Saturday afternoon holiday? Half the world was free to sit back and enjoy itself this sunny afternoon, but he had to spend it pottering about asking questions that led nowhere.

He drove back to Salcott in a state of mental dyspepsia, being only slightly cheered by Dora Siggins. He picked up Dora in the long straight of dull hedged lane that ran for a mile or more parallel to the river just outside the town. In the distance he had taken the plodding figure to be a youth carrying a kit of tools, but as he came nearer and slowed in answer to the raised thumb, he found that it was a girl in dungarees carrying a shopping bag. She grinned cheekily at him and said:

'Saved my life, you have! I missed the bus because I was buying slippers for the dance tonight.'

'Oh,' said Grant, looking at the parcel that had evidently refused to go into the overflowing bag. 'Glass ones?'

'Not me,' she said, banging the door shut behind her and wriggling comfortably into the seat. 'None of that home-by-midnight stuff about me. 'Sides, it wasn't a glass slipper at all, you know. It was fur. French, or something. We learned that at school.'

Grant wondered privately if modern youth had been left any illusions at all. What would a world without fantasy be like? Or did the charming illusion that he was all-important fill for the modern child the place of earlier and more impersonal fantasies? The thought improved his temper considerably.

At least they were quick of wit, these modern children. The cinema, he supposed. It was always the one-and-tuppennys—the regulars—who got the point while the front balcony were still groping. His passenger had got his reference to dance slippers without a second for consideration.

She was a gay child, even after a week's work and missing the bus on a Saturday half-holiday, and poured out her history without any encouragement. Her name was Dora Siggins and she worked at a laundry, but she had a boy friend in a garage at Salcott, and they were going to get married as soon as the boy friend got a rise, which would be at Christmas, if all went as they expected.

When, long afterwards, Grant sent Dora Siggins a box of chocolates as an anonymous tribute to the help she had been to him, he hoped heartily that it would lead to no misunderstanding with the boy friend who was so sure of his rise at Christmas.

'You a commercial?' she asked presently, having exhausted her personal story.

'No,' said Grant. 'I'm a policeman.'

'Go on!' she said, and then, struck by the possibility that he might be telling the truth, took a more careful look at the interior of the car. 'Coo!' she said at length. 'Blamed if you aren't, at that!'

'What convinced you?' Grant said curiously.

'Spit and polish,' she said. 'Only the fire service and the police have the spare time to keep a car shiny this way. I thought the police were forbidden to give lifts?'

'You're thinking of the Post Office, aren't you. Here is Salcott on the horizon. Where do you live?'

'The cottage with the wild cherry tree. My, I can't tell you how glad I am I didn't have to walk those four miles. You got the car out on the fly?'

'No,' Grant said, and asked why she should think that.

'Oh, the plain clothes and all. Thought maybe you

were out for the day on your little own. There's one thing you ought to have that the American police have.'

'What is that?' Grant asked bringing the car to a halt opposite the cottage with the cherry tree.

'Sirens to go yelling along the roads with.'

'God forbid,' Grant said.

'I've always wanted to go tearing along the streets behind a siren, seeing people scattering every way.'

'Don't forget your shoes,' Grant said, unsympathetically, indicating the parcel she was leaving on the seat.

'Oh, gee, no; thanks! Thanks a million for everything. I'll never say a word against the police as long as I live.'

She ran up the cottage path, paused to wave to him, and disappeared.

Grant moved on into the village to resume his questioning.

13

WHEN Grant walked into the Mill House at a quarter to seven he felt that he had riddled Salcott St Mary through a small-meshed sieve, and what he had left in the sieve was exactly nothing. He had had a very fine cross-section of life in England, and he was by that much the richer. But towards solving the problem that had been entrusted to him he had advanced not one foot.

Marta greeted him with her best contralto coo and drew him in to peace and refreshment. The living-room of the Mill House stood over the water, and in the day-time its furnishings swam in the wavering light; a green sub-aqueous light. But this evening Marta had drawn the curtains over the last of the sunset, and shut out the river light; she had prepared a refuge of warmth and reassurance, and Grant, tired and perplexed, was grateful to her.

'I am so glad that it is not Walter who has disappeared,' she said, wafting him to a chair with one of her favourite gestures and beginning to pour sherry.

'Glad?' Grant said, remembering Marta's expressed opinion of Walter.

'If it was Walter who had disappeared, I should be a suspect, instead of a sleeping partner.'

Grant thought that Marta as sleeping partner must have much in common with sleeping dogs.

'As it is I can sit at the side of the law and see the wheels go round. Are you being brilliant, my dear?'

'I'm flummoxed,' Grant said brutally, but Marta took it in her stride.

'You feel that way only because you are tired and hungry; and probably suffering from dyspepsia, anyhow, after having to eat at the White Hart for two days. I'm going to leave you with the sherry decanter and go down and get the wine. Cellar-cooled Moselle. The kitchen is under this room, and the cellar is under the kitchen, and the wine comes up as cold as running water. Oh dear, I promised myself I wasn't going to think of running water any more today. I drew the curtains to shut out the river; I'm not so stuck on the river as I used to be. Perhaps we'll both feel better after the Moselle. When I've brought the wine up from the cellar I'm going to cook you an omelet as only I can cook one, and then we'll settle down. So relax for a little and get back your appetite. If the sherry isn't dry enough for you there's some Tio Pepe in the cupboard; but me, I think it is overrated stuff.'

She went away, and Grant blessed her that she had not plagued him with the questions that must have been crowding her mind. She was a woman who not only appreciated good food and good drink but was possessed of that innate good sense that is half-way to kindness. He had never seen her to better advantage than in this unexpected country home of hers.

He lay back in the lamplight, his feet to the whickering logs, and relaxed. It was warm and very quiet. There was no river song: the Rushmere was a silent stream. No sound at all except the small noises of the fire. On the couch opposite him lay a newspaper, and behind it stood a book-case, but he was too tired to fetch either paper or book. At his elbow was a shelf of reference books. Idly he read the titles till he came to the London telephone book. The sight of those familiar volumes sent his mind flying down a new channel. They had said this evening, when he talked to the Yard, that so far Searle's cousin had not bothered to get in touch with them. They were not surprised by that, of course; the news had broken only that morning, 'and the artist cousin might live anywhere from the Scilly Isles to a farm in Cumberland; she might never read newspapers anyway; she might, if it came to that, be entirely indifferent to any fate that might overtake her cousin. After all, Searle had said quite frankly that they did not care for each other.

But Grant still wanted to talk to someone who knew Searle's background; or at least a little of that background. Now, relaxed and at leisure for the first time in two days, he put out his hand for the S volume, and, on the chance that she lived in London and that she and Searle were the children of two brothers, turned up the Searles. There was a Miss Searle who lived in Holly Pavement, he noticed. Holly Pavement was in Hampstead and was a well-known artist's colony. On an impulse he picked up the telephone and asked for the London number.

'One hour's delay. Call you back,' said the triumphant voice at the other end.

'Priority,' Grant said. And gave his credentials.

'Oh,' said the voice, disappointed but game. 'Oh, well, I'll see what I can do.'

'On the contrary,' Grant said, '*I'll* see what you can do,' and hung up.

He put the telephone book back in its place, and pulled out *Who's Who in the Theatre* to amuse himself with while he waited. Some of it made him feel very old. Actors and actresses he had never heard of already had long lists of successes to their credit. The ones he knew had pages of achievement stretching back into the already-quaint past. He began to look up the people he knew, as one does in the index of an autobiography. Toby Tullis, son of Sydney Tullis and his wife Martha (Speke). It was surprising to think that a national institution like Toby Tullis had ever been subjected to the processes of conception and brought into this world by the normal method. He observed that Toby's early days as an actor were decently shrouded under: 'Was at one time an actor.' His one-time colleagues, Grant knew, would deny with heat that he had ever been even approximately an actor. On the other hand, Grant thought, remembering this morning, his whole life was an 'act'. He had created a part for himself and had played it ever since.

It was surprising, too, to find that Marguerite Merriam (daughter of Geoffrey Merriam and his wife Brenda (Mattson)) had been considerably older than her adolescent fragility had led one to believe. Perhaps if she had lived that adolescent quality would have worn thin, and her power to break the public heart would have declined. That was, no doubt, what Marta had meant when she said that if she had lived another ten years her obituaries would have been back-page stuff.

Marta (daughter of Gervase Wing-Strutt, M.R.C.S.,

L.R.C.P. and his wife Anne (Hallard)) was, of course, entirely orthodox. She had been educated at the best schools and had sneaked her way on to the stage by the back-door of elocution like so many of her well-bred predecessors. Grant hoped that when in the next edition —or at most the next after—the letters D.B.E. followed Marta's name, it would comfort Gervase Wing-Strutt and his wife Anne for being fooled by their daughter a quarter of a century ago.

He had not even taken the cream off the possible entertainment provided by this enchanting volume when the telephone rang.

'Your call to London is through. Will you go ahead, please,' the voice said.

'Hullo,' Grant said. 'Could I speak to Miss Searle?'

'Miss Searle speaking,' said a pleasant voice, a shade on the efficient side.

'Miss Searle, I'm truly sorry to bother you, but have you, by any chance, a cousin called Leslie Searle?'

'I have, and if he has borrowed money from you you are wasting your time if you think that I will pay it back.'

'Oh, no. It is nothing like that. Your cousin has disappeared while staying with friends in the country and we hoped that you might help us to trace him. My name is Grant. I'm a Detective-Inspector at Scotland Yard.'

'Oh,' said the voice, considering but not apparently dismayed. 'Well, I don't see what help I can be to you. Leslie and I never had much to do with each other. He wasn't my cup of tea, and I certainly am not his.'

'It would be some help if I could come and talk to you about him. Would you, perhaps, be at home tomorrow afternoon if I called?'

'Well, tomorrow afternoon I was going to a concert at the Albert Hall.'

'Oh. Then I might manage it just before lunch if that is any better for you.'

'You are very accommodating for a policeman,' she remarked.

'Criminals don't find us that way,' he said.

'I thought providing accommodation for criminals was the end and object of Scotland Yard. It's all right, Inspector. I won't go to the concert. It is not a very good one anyhow.'

'You'll be in if I call?'

'Yes, I'll be here.'

'That is very kind of you.'

'That over-rated photographer didn't take the family jewels with him when he left, did he?'

'No. Oh, no. He has just disappeared.'

She gave a small snort. It was apparent that whatever Miss Searle had to tell him about her cousin there would be no suppression of facts or false modesty in her story.

As Grant hung up, Marta came back preceded by a small boy carrying wood for the fire. The boy put the logs neatly in the hearth, and then eyed Grant with respectful awe.

'Tommy has something he wants to ask you,' Marta said. 'He knows that you are a detective.'

'What is it, Tommy?'

'Will you show me your revolver, sir?'

'I would if I had it with me. But it's in a drawer in Scotland Yard, I'm afraid.'

Tommy looked cut to the heart. 'I thought you always

carried one. The American cops do. You *can* shoot, can't you, sir?'

'Oh, yes,' Grant said relieving the awful fear that was clearly dawning. 'I'll tell you what, next time you come to London, you can come to Scotland Yard and I'll show you the revolver.'

'I can come to the *Yard*? Oh, thank you. Thank you very much, sir. That would be just bonza.'

He went, with a polite goodnight, in an aura of radiance a foot thick.

'And parents think they can cure boys of liking lethal weapons by not giving them toy soldiers,' Marta said, as she set the omelet out on the table. 'Come and eat.'

'I owe you for a trunk call to London.'

'I thought that you were going to relax.'

'I was but I got an idea, and it has taken me the first step forward in this case since I took it over.'

'Good!' she said. 'Now you can feel happy and let your digestive juices do their work.'

A small round table had been set near the fire, with candles for pleasure and decoration, and they ate together in a friendly quiet. Mrs Thrupp came up with the chicken, and was introduced, and was volubly grateful for Grant's invitation to Tommy. After that peace was uninterrupted. Over coffee the talk went to Silas Weekley and the oddness of the ménage in the lane.

'Silas prides himself on living "working-class", whatever that may mean. None of his children is going to begin any better off than he did. He's a frightful bore about his elementary school origins. You would think he was the first elementary schoolboy to go to Oxford since the place was founded. He's the classic case of inverted snobbery.'

'But what does he do with all the money he makes?'

'God knows. Buries it under the floor of that little hut where he works, perhaps. No one is ever allowed to go inside that hut.'

'I interviewed him in that hut this morning.'

'Alan! How clever of you! What was inside?'

'One well-known writer, doing very little work.'

'I expect he sweats blood over his writing. He has no imagination, you know. I mean, he has no idea how another person's mind works. So his situations, and his characters' reaction to the situations, are all clichés. He sells because of his "earthiness", his "elemental strength", God save us all. Let us push back the table and get nearer the fire.'

She opened a cupboard, and said in an excellent imitation of the boys who used to sell things off trays on railway platforms: 'Drambuie, Benedictine, Strega, Grand Marnier, Bols, Chartreuse, Slivovitz, Armagnac, Cognac, Rakia, Kümmel, Various French Sirops of Unspeakable Sweetness, and Mrs Thrupp's Ginger Cordial!'

'Is it your intention to seduce official secrets from the Criminal Investigation Department?'

'No, darling; I am offering homage to your palate. You are one of the few men I know who possesses such a thing.'

She put the Chartreuse and the liqueur glasses on a tray and arranged her long legs in comfort on the couch.

'Now tell me,' she said..

'But I have nothing to tell," he protested.

'I don't mean that kind of tell. I mean talk at me. Pretend I'm your wife—which God forbid—and just make an audience of me. For instance, you don't really think that that poor stick Walter Whitmore ever got up enough red blood to tap the Searle boy on the head, do you?'

'No, I don't think so. Sergeant Williams calls Walter a pushee, and I think I agree with him.'

'Calls him a what?'

Grant explained, and Marta said: 'And how right your Sergeant Williams is! Walter's taking-off is long overdue.'

'He may do his own taking-off if this affair isn't cleared up.'

'Yes, I suppose he *is* having a bad time, poor silly creature. The gossip in a small country place is deadly. Have you had any answer to your police appeal, by the way? I heard it at one o'clock.'

'No, not up to six-forty-five, when I last talked to the Yard. I gave them this number for the next two hours. I hope you don't mind.'

'Why do you think he might have been given a lift?'

'Because if he isn't in the river he must have walked away from it.'

'Of his own accord? But that would be a very odd thing to do.'

'He may be suffering from amnesia. There are five possibilities altogether.'

'Five!'

'On Wednesday night Searle walked away down that lane, healthy and sober; and he has not been near since. The possibilities are: one, that he fell into the water accidentally and was drowned; two, that he was murdered and thrown in the river; three, that he walked away for reasons of his own; four, that he wandered away because he forgot who he was and where he was going; five, that he was kidnapped.'

'Kidnapped!'

'We don't know anything about his American life; we have to make allowances for that. He may even have come to this country to get away from the States for a little. I shan't know about that until we have a report about him from the Coast—if then! Tell me, what did *you* think of Searle?'

'In what way?'

'Well, would you say he was a practical joker, for instance?'

'Anything but.'

'Yes. Liz Garrowby was against that too. She said he wouldn't think a practical joke funny. How impressed do you think he was with Liz Garrowby? You were there to dinner.'

'Impressed enough to make Walter sick with jealousy.'

'Really?'

'They were nice together, Leslie and Liz. They were a natural pair, somehow. Something that Walter and Liz will never be. I don't think Walter knows anything about Liz; and I had an idea that Leslie Searle knew quite a lot.'

'Did you like him when you met him? You took him back with you that night, after dinner.'

'Yes. Yes to both. I liked him with reservations.'

'What kind of reservations?'

'It's difficult to describe. I could hardly take my eyes

off him, and yet he never struck me as being—real. That sounds mad, doesn't it.'

'You mean there was something phony about him?'

'Not in the accepted sense. He was obviously what he said he was. In any case, our Miss Easton-Dixon bears witness to that, as you probably know.'

'Yes, I was talking to Miss Easton-Dixon this afternoon about him. Her photograph of him may prove very useful. What did you and Searle talk about, the night you brought him back with you?'

'Oh, cabbages and kings. People he had photographed. People we had both met. People he wanted to meet. We spent a long time in mutual adoring of Danny Minsky, and another long time in furious disagreement about Marguerite Merriam. Like everyone else he thought Marguerite the world's genius, and wouldn't hear a word against her. I got so annoyed with him that I told him a few home-truths about Marguerite. I was ashamed of myself afterwards. It's a mean thing to break children's toys.'

'I expect it did him good. He was too old to have the facts of life kept from him.'

'I hear you've been collecting alibis today.'

'How did you hear?'

'The way I hear everything. From· Mrs Thrupp. Who are the unlucky people who have none?'

'Practically the whole village, including Miss Easton-Dixon.'

'Our Dixie is "out". Who else?'

'Miss Lavinia Fitch.'

'*Dear* Lavinia!' Marta said, laughing outright at the thought of Miss Fitch on murder bent.

'Liz Garrowby?'

'Poor Liz must be having a thin time over this. I think she was half in love with the boy.'

'Mrs Garrowby?'

Marta paused to consider this. 'Do you know, I wouldn't put it past the woman. She would do it and not turn a hair because she would persuade herself that it was the right thing to do. She'd even go to church afterwards and ask God's blessing on it.'

'Toby Tullis?'

'N-o, I hardly think so. Toby would find some other way of getting even. Something much less risky for Toby and just as satisfying. Toby is fertile in inventing small revenges. I don't think he would need to murder anyone.'

'Silas Weekley?'

'I wonder. I wonder. Yes, I think Silas would commit murder. Especially if the book he happened to be writing at the moment was not going well. The books are Silas's outlet for his hatred, you see. If that was dammed up he might kill someone. Someone who seemed to him rich and well-favoured and undeservedly fortunate.'

'You think Weekley mad?'

'Oh, yes. Not certifiable perhaps, but definitely unbalanced. Is there any truth, by the way, in the rumour of a quarrel between Walter and the Searle boy?'

'Whitmore denies that it was a quarrel. He says it was "just a spat".'

'So there *was* bad feeling between them?'

'I don't know if we have even evidence for that. A temporary annoyance is hardly the same thing as bad feeling. Men can disagree quite fundamentally in a pub of an evening without any fundamental bad feeling on either side.'

'Oh, you are maddening. Of course there was bad feeling, and of course we know why. It was about Liz.'

'Having no connections in the Fourth Dimension, I couldn't say,' Grant said, mocking her jumped-to conclusion. 'Whitmore said Searle was "provocative". What, can you tell me from your point of vantage, would he be provocative about?'

'He probably told Walter how little he appreciated Liz, and that if Walter didn't mend his ways he would take Liz from him, and if Walter thought he wasn't up to it he was wrong and he would get Liz to pack and walk away with him by a week next Tuesday, and there was five pounds that said he was right. And Walter said, very huffy and stiff, that in this country we did not bet on the possible bestowal of women's favours, at least gentlemen didn't, and to put five pounds on Liz was simply insulting (Walter has no sense of the ridiculous at all, you know; that is how he perpetrates those broadcasts and endears himself to old ladies who avoid the country like the plague and wouldn't know a wren if they saw one); and Leslie probably said that if he thought a fiver too little he was willing to make it ten, since if Liz had been engaged to a prig like Walter for nearly twelve months she was just ripe for a change and the ten would be just found money, and so then Walter got up and went out and banged the door behind him.'

'How did you know about the banged door?'

'My dear soul, everyone in Orfordshire knows about the banged door by this time. That is why Walter is suspect Number One. Is that all your list of Lacking Alibis, by the way?'

'No, there is Serge Ratoff.'

'Oh. What was Serge doing?'

'Dancing on the greensward by the river in the dark.'

'That has the ring of truth, anyhow.'

'Why? Have you seen him?'

'No. But it is just the kind of thing Serge would do. He is still full of the idea of a come-back, you know. Before the scene about Leslie Searle, he was planning the come-back as a way of pleasing Toby; now he is planning it just to "show" Toby.'

'Where do you get all this inside knowledge?'

'I haven't played parts for twenty-five years on just the producer's directions,' she said.

He looked across at her, elegant and handsome in the firelight, and thought of all the different parts that he had seen her play: courtesans and frustrated hags, careerists and domestic doormats. It was true that actors had a perception, an understanding of human motive, that normal people lacked. It had nothing to do with intelligence, and very little to do with education. In general knowledge Marta was as deficient as a not very bright child of eleven; her attention automatically slid off anything that was alien to her own immediate interests and the result was an almost infantine ignorance. He had seen the same thing in hospital nurses, and sometimes in overworked G.P.s. But put a script in her hands, and from a secret and native store of knowledge she drew the wherewithal to build her characterisation of the author's creation.

'Supposing that this really is a case of homicide,' he

said. 'Judging entirely on looks and recent form, so to speak, who would you put your money on?'

She considered this for a little, turning her empty liqueur glass in the firelight.

'Emma Garrowby, I think,' she said at last. 'Could Emma have done it? Physically speaking, I mean.'

'Yes. She left Miss Easton-Dixon where their ways parted on Wednesday night, and after that time was her own. No one knows what time she came back to Trimmings. The others had gone to bed; or rather, to their rooms. It is Mrs Garrowby who locks up the front of the house, anyhow.'

'Yes. Ample time. It isn't so very far from Trimmings to that bend in the river. I do wonder what Emma's shoes were like on Thursday morning. Or did she clean them herself.'

'Believe me, if there was any unwonted mud on the shoes she cleaned them herself. Mrs Garrowby looks to me a very methodical person. Why do you pick on Emma Garrowby?'

'Well, I take it you commit murder because you are one-idea'd. Or have become one-idea'd. As long as you have a variety of interests you can't care about any one of them to the point of murder. It is when you have all your eggs in the same basket, or only one egg left in the basket, that you lose your sense of proportion. Do I make myself clear, Inspector Grant?'

'Perfectly.'

'Good. Have some more Chartreuse. Well, Emma seems to me the most concentrated of the possible suspects. No one could call Serge concentrated, except on the thing of the moment. Serge spends his life having flaring rows, and has never shown signs of killing anyone. The farthest he ever gets is to fling whatever happens to come handiest.'

'Lacking a whip,' Grant said; and told her of his interview with Serge. 'And Weekley?'

'On form, to use your own excellent metaphor, Silas is only a pound or two behind Emma; but quite definitely behind. Silas has his own success, his family, the books he is going to write in the future (even if they are just the same old ones over again in different words); Silas's interest isn't *channelled* the way Emma's is. Short of having a brain-storm, some unreasoning hatred, Silas would have no urge to get rid of Leslie. Nor would Toby. Toby's life simply corruscates with variety. Toby would never think of killing anyone. As I told you, he has too many other ways of making the score even. But Emma. Emma has nothing but Liz.'

She thought it over for a moment, and Grant let the silence lie uninterrupted.

'You should have seen Emma when Walter and Liz announced their engagement,' she said at last. 'She— she positively *glittered*. She was a walking Christmas tree. It was what she had always wanted, and against all probability it had happened. Walter, who met all the clever and beautiful women of this generation, had fallen in love with Liz and they were going to be married. Walter would get Trimmings one day, and Lavinia's fortune, so even if his vogue went they would have as much of this world's goods as anyone could possibly want or use. It was a fairy-tale come true. She was floating just an inch or two off the ground. Then Leslie Searle came.'

Marta, the actress, let the silence come back. And being also an artist she left it unbroken.

The logs slipped and spluttered, sending up fresh jets of flame, and Grant lay still in his chair and thought about Emma Garrowby.

And about the two things that Marta did not know.

It was odd that Marta's chosen suspect should occupy the same area as the two unaccountables in this case: the glove in Searle's drawer, and the space in the photographic box.

Emma. Emma Garrowby. The woman who had brought up a younger sister and when that sister moved out from under her wing married a widower with a young child. She channelled her interest as naturally as Toby Tullis spread his wide, didn't she? She had been radiant—'a walking Christmas tree'—over the engagement; and in the period since that engagement (it was five months, he happened to know, not twelve) her initial delight must have spread and amplified to something much more formidable; an acceptance; a sense of achievement, of security. The engagement had stood whatever small shocks it had encountered in these five months, and Emma must have got used to thinking of it as safe and immutable.

And then, as Marta said, Leslie Searle.

Searle with his charm and his fly-by-night life. Searle with his air of being not quite of this world. No one could view this modern shower of gold with more instant distrust than Emma Garrowby.

'What would fit into a space 10¼ inches, by 3½ by 4?' he asked.

'A hair brush,' said Marta.

172

There was a game played by psychologists, Grant remembered, where the victim said the first thing that occurred to him on hearing a given word. It must work out pretty well, all things considered. He had put this same proposition to Bill Maddox, and Maddox, as unhesitatingly as Marta had said 'A hairbrush', had said 'A spanner'. He remembered that Williams had proffered a bar of soap.

'Anything else?'

'A set of dominoes. A box of envelopes? No, a shade on the small side. Packs of cards? Enough cards to set up on a desert island! Table cutlery. The family spoons. Someone been secreting the family silver?'

'No. It is just something I wondered about.'

'If it's the Trimmings silver, just let it go, my dear. It wouldn't fetch thirty shillings the lot at an auction sale.' Her eye went in unconscious satisfaction to the Georgian simplicity of her own implements on the table behind her. 'Tell me, Alan, it wouldn't be indiscreet or unprofessional, would it, to tell me who is your own favourite for the part?'

'The part?'

'The killer.'

'It would be both unprofessional and indiscreet. But I don't think there is any wild indiscretion in telling you that I don't think there is one.'

'What! You really think Leslie Searle is still alive? Why?'

Why indeed, he asked himself. What was there in the set-up that gave him this feeling of being at a performance? Of being pushed into the stalls so that an orchestra pit intervened between him and reality. The Assistant

173

Commissioner had once said to him in an unwonted moment of expansiveness that he had the most priceless of all attributes for his job: flair. 'But don't let it ride you, Grant,' he had said. 'Keep your eye on the evidence.' Was this a sample of letting his flair ride him? The chances were ninety-nine to one that Searle had fallen into the river. All the evidence pointed that way. If it hadn't been for the complication of the quarrel with Whitmore, he, Grant, would not have entered into the affair at all; it would have been a simple case of 'missing believed drowned'.

And yet. And yet. Now you see it, now you don't. That old conjurer's phrase. It haunted him.

Half consciously he said it aloud.

Marta stared and said: 'A conjuring trick? By whom? For what?'

'I don't know. I just have a strong feeling that I'm being taken for a ride!'

'You think that Leslie just walked away somehow?'

'Or someone planned it to look like that. Or something. I have a strong feeling of watching something being sawn in half.'

'You're overworking,' Marta said. 'Where do you think Leslie could have disappeared to? Unless he just came back to the village and lay doggo somewhere.'

Grant came wide awake and regarded her with admiration. 'Oddly enough,' he said, amused, 'I had never thought of that. Do you think Toby is hiding him to make things difficult for Walter?'

'No, I know it doesn't make sense. But neither does your idea about his walking away. Where would he walk to in the middle of the night in nothing but flannels and a raincoat?'

'I shall know more about that when I have seen his cousin tomorrow.'

'He has a cousin? How surprising. It's like finding Mercury with an in-law. Who is he?'

'It's a woman. A painter, I understand. A delightful creature who has given up an Albert Hall Sunday afternoon concert to be at home for me. I used your telephone to make an assignation with her.'

'And you expect her to know why Leslie walked away in the middle of the night in nothing but flannels and a raincoat?'

'I expect her to be able to suggest where Leslie might have been headed for.'

'To borrow the callboy's immortal phrase: I hope it keeps fine for you,' Marta said.

14

GRANT drove back to Wickham through the spring night, cheered in body and soul.

And Emma Garrowby sat beside him all the way.

Flair might whisper soft seductions to him, but Emma was there in the middle of the picture, where Marta had set her, and she was much too solid to be conjured away. Emma made sense. Emma was example and precedent. The classic samples of ruthlessness were domestic. The Lizzie Bordons. Emma, if it came to that, was primordial. A female creature protecting its young. It required immense ingenuity to find a reason why Leslie Searle should have chosen to disappear. It needed no ingenuity at all to suggest why Emma Garrowby should have killed him.

In fact, it was a sort of perversity to keep harking back to the idea that Searle might have ducked. He could just hear the A.C. if he ever came before him with a theory like that. Evidence, Grant, suggestive evidence. Common sense, Grant, common sense. Don't let your flair ride you, Grant, don't let your flair ride you. Disappear of his own accord? This happy young man who could pay his bills at the Westmorland, buy expensive clothes to wear and expensive sweets to give away, travel the world at other people's expense? This young man of such surprising good-looks that every head he encountered was turned either literally or metaphorically? This charming young man who liked plain little Liz so much that he kept a glove of hers? This professionally successful young man who was engaged in a deal that would bring him both money and kudos?

Common sense, Grant. Evidence, Grant. Don't let your flair ride you.

Consider Emma Garrowby, Grant. She had the opportunity. She had the motive. And, on form, she probably had the will. She knew where the camp was that night.

But she didn't know that they had come in to Salcott for a drink.

He wasn't drowned in Salcott.

She couldn't have known that she would find him alone. It was sheer chance that they separated that night.

Someone found him alone. Why not Emma?

How could it happen?

Perhaps she arranged it.

Emma! How?

Has it struck you that Searle engineered that exit of Walter's?

No. How?

It was Searle who was provocative. He provoked Walter to the point where he couldn't stand it a minute longer, and had either to go or stay and have a row. Searle got rid of Walter that evening.

Why should he?

Because he had an appointment.

An appointment! With whom?

Liz Garrowby.

That is absurd. There is no evidence whatever that the Garrowby girl had any serious interest in——

Oh, it was not Liz who sent Searle the message to meet her.

No? Who then?

Emma.

You mean that Searle went to meet someone he thought was Liz?

Yes. He behaved like a lover, if you think about it.

How?

Do you remember how he took farewell of his acquaintances that night? The banter about going to their beds on so fine a spring night? The gaiety? The on-top-of-the-worldness?

He had just had several beers.

So had his companions. Some of them a great deal more than several. But were they singing metaphorical songs to the spring night? They were not. They were taking the shortest cut home to bed, even the youngest of them.

Well, it's a theory.

It is more than that. It is a theory in accordance with the evidence.

Evidence, Grant, evidence.

Don't let your flair ride you, Grant.

All the way along the dark lanes between Salcott St Mary and Wickham, Emma Garrowby sat beside him. And when he went to bed he took her with him.

Because he was tired, and had dined well, and had at last seen a path of some kind open in front of him, he slept well. And when his eyes opened in daylight on THE HOUR COMETH in purple wool cross-stitch, he regarded the text as a promise rather than a warning. He looked forward to going to town, if only as a mental bath after his plunge into Salcott St Mary. He could then come back and see it in proportion. You couldn't get the flavour of anything properly unless you cleaned your palate between times. He had wondered often how married men managed to combine their domestic lives with the absorbing demands of police work. It occurred to him now for the first time that married life must be the perfect palate-cleanser. There could be nothing like a spell of helping young Bobby with his algebra to bring you back with a fresh mind to the problem of the current crime.

At least he would be able to get some clean shirts, he thought. He put his things into his bag, and turned to go down to breakfast. It was Sunday and still early, but they would manage to give him something. As he opened the door of his room the telephone rang.

The White Hart's only concession to progress was to install bedside telephones. He crossed the room to the instrument and picked it up.

'Inspector Grant?' said the voice of the landlord. 'Just a minute please; you're wanted on the phone.' There was a moment's silence, and then he said: 'Go ahead, please; you're through.

'Hullo.'

'Alan?' said Marta's voice. 'Is that you, Alan?'

'Yes, it's me. You're awake early aren't you?'

'Listen, Alan. Something has happened. You must come out straight away.'

'Out? To Salcott, you mean?'

'To the Mill House. Something has happened. It's very important or I wouldn't have called you so early.'

'But what has happened? Can't you——'

'You're on a hotel telephone, aren't you.'

'Yes.'

'I can't very well tell you, Alan. Something has turned up. Something that alters everything. Or rather, everything you—you believed in, so to speak.'

'Yes. All right. I'll come at once.'

'Have you had breakfast?'

'Not yet.'

'I'll have some ready for you.'

What a woman, he thought as he put back the receiver. He had always thought that the first requisite in a wife was intelligence, and now he was sure of it. There was no room in his life for Marta, and none in her life for him; but it was a pity, all the same. A woman who could announce a surprising development in a homicide case without babbling on the telephone was a prize, but one who could in the same breath ask if he had had breakfast and arrange to supply him with the one he had not had was above rubies.

He went to collect his car, full of speculation. What could Marta possibly have unearthed? Something that Searle had left the night he was there? Some piece of gossip that the milkman had brought?

One thing was certain: it was not a body. If it had been a body Marta, being Marta, would have conveyed as much, so that he could bring out with him all the necessary paraphernalia and personnel to deal with such a discovery.

It was a day of high wind and rainbows. The halcyon time of windless sunlight that comes each year to the English spring when the first dust lies on the roads was over. Spring was all of a sudden wild and robust. Glittering showers slanted across the landscape. Great clouds soared up over the horizon and swept in shrieking squalls across the sky. The trees cowered, and plumed themselves, and cowered again.

The countryside was deserted. Not because of the weather but because it was Sunday. Some of the cottages, he observed, still had their blinds drawn. People who got up at the crack of dawn during the week, and had no animals to get them up on Sunday, must be glad to sleep late. He had grumbled often when his police duties had broken into his private life (a luxury grumble, since he could have retired years ago when his aunt left him her money), but to spend one's life in bondage to the predilections of animals must be a sad waste of a free man's time.

As he brought the car up to the landward side of the Mill House, where the door was, Marta came out to greet him. Marta never 'dressed the part' in the country as so many of her colleagues did. She looked on the country rather as the country people themselves did, as a place to be lived in; not something that one put on specially bright and casual clothes for. If her hands were cold she wore gloves. She did not feel that she must look like a gypsy just because she happened to live in the Mill House at Salcott St Mary. She was therefore looking as chic and sophisticated this morning as though she were receiving him on the steps of Stanworth. But he thought she had a shocked look. Indeed she looked as though she had quite lately been very sick.

'Alan! You can't imagine how glad I was to hear your voice on the telephone. I was afraid that you might have gone to town, early as it was.'

'What is this that has turned up so unexpectedly?' he asked making for the door. But she led him round and down to the kitchen door at the side of the house.

'It was your follower, Tommy Thrupp, that found it. Tommy is mad on fishing. And he quite often goes out before breakfast to fish, because apparently that is a good time.' The 'apparently' was typically Marta, he thought. Marta had lived by the river for years and still had to take someone else's word about the proper time for fishing. 'On Sundays he usually takes something in his pocket and doesn't come back—something to eat, I mean—but this morning he came back inside an hour because he had—because he had caught something very odd.'

She opened the bright green door and led him into the kitchen. In the kitchen were Tommy Thrupp and his mother. Mrs Thrupp was huddled over the stove as if she also was feeling not too well, but Tommy came to meet them in sparkling form. There was nothing sickly about Tommy. Tommy was transfigured. He was translated. He was six feet high and crowned with lightning.

'Look, sir! Look what I fished up!' he said, before Marta could say anything, and drew Grant to the kitchen table. On the table, carefully placed on several thicknesses of newspaper so as to preserve the scrubbed perfection of the wood, was a man's shoe.

'I'll never be able to bake on that table again,' moaned Mrs Thrupp, not looking round.

Grant glanced at the shoe and remembered the police description of the missing man's clothes.

'It's Searle's, I take it,' he said.

'Yes,' Marta said.

It was a brown shoe, and instead of being laced it was tied with a buckle and strap across the instep. It was water-logged and very muddy.

'Where did you fish it up, Tommy?'

"Bout a hundred yards down-stream from the big bend.'

'I suppose you didn't think of marking the place?'

'A course I marked it!' Tommy said, hurt.

'Good for you. Presently you'll have to show me the place. Meanwhile wait here, will you. Don't go out and talk about this.'

'No, sir, I won't. No one's in on this but me and the police.'

A little brightened by this version of the situation, Grant went upstairs to the telephone in the living-room and called Inspector Rodgers. After some delay, since the station had to connect him to the Rodgers' home, he was put through to him, and broke the news that the river would have to be dragged again and why.

'Oh, lord!' groaned Rodgers. 'Did the Thrupp boy say where he fished it up?'

'About a hundred yards down from the big bend, if that conveys anything to you.'

'Yes. That's about two hundred yards down-stream from where they had their bivouac. We did that stretch with a small-tooth comb. You don't think that per-haps——? Does the shoe look as if it had been in the water since Wednesday night?'

'It does indeed.'

'Oh, well. I'll make arrangements. It would happen on a Sunday, wouldn't it?'

'Do it as quietly as you can, will you? We don't want more spectators than we can help.'

As he hung up Marta came in with a tray and began to put his breakfast on the table.

'Mrs Thrupp is still what she calls "heaving", so I judged it better to do your breakfast myself. How do you like your eggs? Sunny side up?'

'If you really want to know, I like them broken when they are half cooked and rummelled up with a fork.'

'*Panaché!*' Marta said, delighted. 'That is one I have not met before. We are growing intimate, aren't we! I am probably the only woman alive except your house-keeper who knows that you like your breakfast eggs streaky. Or—am I?'

'Well, there's a woman in a village near Amiens that I once confessed it to. But I doubt if she would remember.'

'She is probably making a fortune out of the idea. Eggs *à l'Anglaise* probably has a totally new meaning in France nowadays. Brown bread or white?'

'Brown, please. I'm going to have to owe you for another trunk call.' He picked up the telephone again and called Williams's home address in London. While he waited for the connection he called Trimmings and asked to speak to the housekeeper. When Mrs Brett a little breathless, arrived on the wire he asked who was in the habit of cleaning the shoes at Trimmings and was told that it was the kitchen girl, Polly.

'Could you find out from Polly whether Mr Searle was in the habit of taking off his brown buckled shoes without unbuckling them, or if he always unbuckled them first?'

Yes, Mrs Brett would do that, but wouldn't the Inspector like to speak to Polly himself?

'No, thank you. I'll confirm anything she says, later on, of course. But I think she is less likely to get flustered if you ask her a quite ordinary question than if she was brought to the telephone to be questioned by a stranger. I don't want her to be agitated into thinking about the question at all. I want her first natural reaction to the question. Were the shoes buckled or unbuckled when she cleaned them?'

Mrs Brett understood, and would the Inspector hang on?

'No. I'm expecting an important call. But I shall call you back in a very short time.'

Then London came on the wire, and Williams's not-too-pleased voice could be heard telling the Exchange: 'All right, all right, I've been ready any time this last five minutes.'

'That you, Williams? This is Grant. Listen. I was coming up to town today to interview Leslie Searle's cousin. Yes, I found out where she lived. Her name is Searle. Miss Searle. And she lives at 9 Holly Pavement, in Hampstead. It's a sort of coagulation of artists. I talked to her last night on the telephone and I arranged to see her this afternoon about three. Now I can't. A boy has just fished a shoe belonging to Leslie Searle out of the river. Yes, all right, crow! So we have to start dragging all over again, and I have to be here. Are you free to go and see Miss Searle for me, or shall I get someone else from the Yard?'

'No, I'll go, sir. What do you want me to ask her?'

'Get everything she knows about Leslie Searle. When she saw him last. What friends he had in England. Everything she can give you about him.'

'Very good. What time shall I call you back?'

'Well, you ought to be there at a quarter to three, and leaving an hour clear—four o'clock, perhaps.'

'At the Wickham station?'

'Well, no, perhaps not. In view of the slowness of dragging, perhaps you had better call me at the Mill House at Salcott. It is Salcott 5.'

It was only when he had hung up that he realised that he had not asked Williams how his mission to Benny Skoll had turned out.

Marta came in with his breakfast, and as she poured his coffee he talked to Trimmings again.

Mrs Brett had talked to Polly, and Polly had no doubt about the matter at all. The straps on Mr Searle's brown shoes had always been undone when he put them out for cleaning. She knew because she used to rebuckle them so as to keep the straps from banging about when she cleaned them. She buckled them to keep the straps still and unbuckled them when she had finished.

So that was that.

He began to eat his breakfast, and Marta poured out a cup of coffee for herself and sat sipping it. She looked cold and pale, but he could not resist the question:

'Did you notice anything odd about the shoe?'

'Yes. It hadn't been unfastened.'

A marvellous woman. He supposed that she must have vices to counterbalance so many excellences but he couldn't imagine what they could be.

15

It was very cold by the river. The willows shivered, and the water was pewter colour, its surface alternately wrinkled by the wind and pitted by the passing showers. As the slow hours went by Rodgers's normally anxious face slipped into a settled melancholy, and the tip of his nose peering out from the turned-up collar of his waterproof was pink and sad. So far no intruders had come to share their vigil. The Mill House had been sworn to secrecy and had not found the secrecy any strain; · Mrs Thrupp had retired to bed, still 'heaving'; and Tommy, as police ally, was part of the dragging party. The wide sweep of the river across the alluvial land was far from road or path and devoid of dwellings, so there were no passers-by to stop and stare, to pause for a little and then go on to spread the news.

They were in a world by themselves down there by the river. A timeless world, and comfortless.

Grant and Rodgers had exhausted professional post-mortems long ago, and had got no further. Now they were just two men alone in a meadow on a chilly spring day. They sat together on the stump of a fallen willow, Grant watching the slow sweep of the questing drag, Rodgers looking out across the wide flats of the valley floor.

'This is all flooded in winter,' he said. 'Looks quite lovely, too, if you could forget the damage it's doing.'

' "Swift beauty come to pass
     Has drowned the blades that strove",'
Grant said.

'What is that?'

'What an army friend of mine wrote about floods.

    "Where once did wake and move
      The slight and ardent grass,
      Swift beauty come to pass
      Has drowned the blades that strove." '

'Nice,' Rodgers said.

'Sadly old-fashioned,' Grant said. 'It *sounds* like poetry. A fatal defect, I understand.'

'Is it long?'

'Just two verses and the moral.'

'What is the moral?'

    ' "O Final Beauty, found
      In many a drowned place,
      We love not less thy face
      For lesser beauties drowned." '

Rodgers thought it over. 'That's good, that is,' he said. 'Your army friend knew what he was talking about. I was never one for reading poems in books—I mean collections, but magazines sometimes put verses in to fill up the space when a story doesn't come to the bottom of the page. You know?'

'I know.'

'I read a lot of these, and every now and then one of them rings a bell. I remember one of them to this day. It wasn't poetry properly speaking, I mean it didn't rhyme, but it got me where I lived. It said:

"My lot is cast in inland places,
Far from sounding beach
And crying gull,
And I
Who knew the sea's voice from my babyhood
Must listen to a river purling
Through green fields,
And small birds gossiping
Among the leaves."

'Now, you see, I was bred by the sea, over at Mere Harbour, and I've never quite got used to being away from it. You feel hedged in, suffocated. But I never found the words for it till I read that. I know exactly how that bloke felt. "Small birds gossiping!" '

The scorn and exasperation in his voice amused Grant, but something amused him much more and he began to laugh.

'What's funny?' Rodgers asked, a shade defensively.

'I was just thinking how shocked the writers of slick detective stories would be if they could witness two police inspectors sitting on a willow tree swapping poems.'

'Oh, them!' Rodgers said, in the tone that in lower circles is followed by a spit. 'Ever read any of these things?'

'Oh, yes. Now and then.'

'My sergeant makes a hobby of it. Collects the howlers. His record so far is ninety-two to a book. In a thing called *Gods to the Rescue* by some woman or other.' He stopped to watch something and added: 'There's a woman coming now. Pushing a bike.'

Grant took a look and said: 'That's not a woman. It's a goddess to the rescue.'

It was the unconquerable Marta, with vacuum flasks of hot coffee and sandwiches for all.

'The bicycle was the only way I could think of for carrying them,' she explained, 'but it is difficult'because most of the gates don't open.'

'How did you get through them, then?'

'I unloaded the bicycle, lifted the thing over, and loaded it again the other side.'

'The spirit that made the Empire.'

'That's as may be, but Tommy must come with me on the way back, and help me.'

'Sure I will, Miss Hallard,' Tommy said, his mouth full of sandwich.

The men came up from the river and were presented to Marta. It amused Grant to notice the *cameraderie* of those who quite patently had never heard of her, and the awed good manners of those who had.

'I think the news has leaked out,' Marta said. 'Toby rang me up and asked if it was true that the river was being dragged again.'

'You didn't tell him why?'

'No. Oh, no,' she said, her face going a little bleak again at the memory of the shoe.

By two o'clock in the afternoon they had a large attendance. And by three o'clock the place was like a fair, with the local constable making valiant efforts to preserve some kind of decency.

At half-past three, when they had dragged the river almost as far as Salcott itself and had still turned up nothing, Grant went back to the Mill House and found Walter Whitmore there.

'It was kind of you to send us the message, Inspector,' he said. 'I should have come to the river, but somehow I couldn't.'

'There was not the slightest need for you to come.'

'Marta said that you were coming back here at tea-time, so I waited here. Any—results?'

'Not so far.'

'Why did you want to know about the shoe, this morning?'

'Because it was fastened when found. I wanted to know if Searle normally pulled off those shoes without unbuckling them. Apparently he always unbuckled them.'

'Then why—how could the shoe be fastened now?'

'Either it was sucked off by the current, or he kicked it off to make swimming easier.'

'I see,' Walter said, drearily.

He refused tea, and went away looking more disorientated than ever.

'I do wish I could be as sorry for him as I should be,' Marta said. 'China or Indian?'

Grant had had three large cups of scalding tea ('So bad for your inside!' Marta said) and was beginning to feel human again, when Williams rang to report.

The report, in spite of Williams's best endeavours, was meagre. Miss Searle didn't like her cousin and made no bones about it. She, too, was an American, but they had been born at opposite sides of the United States and had never met until they were grown up. They had fought at sight, apparently. He sometimes rang her up when he came to England, but not this time. She had not known that he was in England.

Williams had asked her if she was out a lot, and if she thought it possible that Searle could have called, or telephoned, and not found her. She said that she had been in the Highlands, painting, and that Searle might have called her many times without her knowledge. When she was away the studio was empty and there was no one to take telephone messages.

'Did you see the paintings?' Grant asked. 'The ones of Scotland.'

'Oh, yes. The place was full of them.'

'What were they like?'

'Very like Scotland.'

'Oh, orthodox.'

'I wouldn't know. The west of Sutherland and Skye, mostly.'

'And about his friends in this country?'

'She said she was surprised to hear that he had any friends anywhere.'

'She didn't suggest to you that Searle was a wrong 'un?'

'No, sir. Nothing like that.'

'And she couldn't suggest any reason why he should suddenly disappear, or where he could disappear to?'

'No, she couldn't. He has no people, she did tell me that. Parents dead, apparently; and he was an only child. But about his friends she seemed to know nothing. What he said about having only a cousin in England was true, anyhow.'

'Well, thank you very much, Williams. I quite forgot to ask you this morning if you found Benny?'

'Benny? Oh, yes. Quite easily.'

'And did he cry?'

Grant heard Williams laugh.

'No. He pulled a new one this time. He pretended to faint.'

'What did that get him?'

'It got him three free brandies and the sympathy of the multitude. We were in a pub, I need hardly say. After the second brandy he began to come to and moan about the way he was being persecuted, so they gave him a third. I was very unpopular.'

Grant considered this a fine sample of understatement.

'Luckily it was a West End pub,' Williams said. This, being translated, meant that there was no actual interference with his performance of his duty.

'Did he agree to go with you for questioning?'

'He said he would go if I let him telephone first. I said he knew quite well that he was free to telephone anyone at any hour of the day or night—that was a Post Office arrangement—but if his call was innocent I supposed he didn't mind my being the fly on the telephone-booth wall.'

'And did he agree?'

'He practically dragged me into the box. And who do you think that little bastard was telephoning to?'

'His M.P.?'

'No. I think M.P.s are a bit shy of him nowadays. He overstayed his welcome last time. No, he rang up some bloke he knows who writes for the *Watchman* and told him the tale. Said he was no sooner "out" than some policeman or other was on his tail wanting him to go to Scotland Yard for questioning, and how was a man to go straight if he was having an innocent drink with his friends who didn't know anything about him, and an obvious plain-clothes tec came up and wanted to speak to him, and so on and so on. Then he came with me, quite pleased with himself.'

'Was he any help to the Yard?'

'No, but his girl was.'

'Did she blab?'

'No, she was wearing Poppy's earrings. Poppy Plumtre's.'

'No!'

'If we didn't happen to be taking Benny out of circulation for a little, I think his girl would put him out of it for good. She's raving mad. He hasn't had her very long, and it seems she was thinking of leaving him, so Benny "bought" her a pair of diamond earrings. The amount of intelligence Benny has wouldn't inconvenience a ladybird.'

'Did you get the rest of Poppy's stuff?'

'Yes. Benny coughed up. He hadn't had time to get to a fence with them.'

'Good work. What about the *Watchman*?'

'Well, I did want to let that *Watchman* bit of silliness stew in his own juice. But the Super wouldn't let me. Said it was no good having trouble that we could avoid even if we had the pleasure of seeing the *Watchman* making a fool of itself. So I had to ring him up and tell him.'

'At least you must have got something back out of that.'

'Oh, yes. Yes. I don't deny I got some kick out of that. I said: "Mr Ritter, I'm Detective-Sergeant Williams. I was present when Benny Skoll rang you up a few hours ago." "You were *present*?" he said. "But he was lodging a complaint against you!" "Oh, yes," I said. "It's a free country you know." "I don't call it so free for some," he said. "You were dragging him away to be questioned at Scotland Yard." I said I invited him to accompany me, and he didn't have to if he didn't want to.

'Then he gave me the old spiel about hounding criminals, and Benny Skoll having paid his debt to Society, and that we had no right to hound him now that he was a free man again, and so forth. "You have shamed him before his friends," says Mr Ritter, "and pushed him back to hopelessness. How much the better is Scotland Yard for having badgered poor little Benny Skoll this afternoon?"

' "Two thousand pounds worth," I said.

' "What?" he said. "What are you talking about?"

' "That is the amount of jewellery he stole from Poppy Plumtre's flat on Friday night."

' "How do you know it was Benny?" he asked.

'I said Benny had handed over the loot in person, with the exception of two large single diamond earrings which were gracing the ears of his current lady friend. Then I said: "*Good*night, sir", very sweet and low, the way they do in the Children's Hour, and hung up. You know, I think he had already written that letter about poor innocent Benny. He was so dashed. Writers must feel very flat when they've written something that no one can use.'

'Wait till Mr Ritter's flat is burgled,' Grant said. 'He'll come to us screaming for the criminal's blood.'

'Yes, sir. Funny, isn't it? They're always the worst

when it happens to themselves. Any word from San Francisco?'

'Not yet, but it may come any minute. It doesn't seem so important now.'

'No. When I think of the whole notebook I filled interviewing bus conductors in Wickham! No good for anything but the wastepaper basket.'

'*Never* throw notes away, Williams.'

'Keep them for seven years and find a use for them?'

'Keep them for your autobiography, if you like, but keep them. I would like to have you back here, but at the moment the work doesn't warrant it. It is just a matter of standing about in the cold.'

'Well, I hope something turns up before sunset, sir.'

'I hope it does. Literally.'

Grant hung up and went back to the river-bank. The crowd had thinned a little as people began to go home to their Sunday high-tea, but the solid core who would happily starve in order to see a man's dead body dragged from the river were still there. Grant looked at their blue moronic faces and speculated for the thousandth time since he became a policeman about what made them tick. One thing was certain; if we revived public executions tomorrow, the 'gate' would be of cup-tie proportions.

Rodgers had gone back to Wickham, but it seemed that the Press had arrived; both the local man and the Crome correspondent of the London dailies wanted to know why the river was being re-dragged. There was also the Oldest Inhabitant. The Oldest Inhabitant had a nose and chin that approximated so closely that Grant wondered how he shaved. He was a vain old party but he was the representative in this gathering of something more powerful than any of them: Race Memory; and as such was to be respected.

'No use you draggin' any furner'n the village,' he said to Grant, as one giving the under-gardener instructions.

'No?'

'No. No use. She lets everything down, there. Down into the mud.'

'She' was evidently the river.

'Why?'

'She go slow there. Tired, like. Drops everything. Then when she be round the turn, half-way to Wickham there, she go tearing off agin all light and happy. Ah. That is what she do. Drops everything she be carrying into the mud, and then she go quiet for a little, lookin' round t'see if people notice what she done, then woops! she be off to Wickham at the tear.' He cocked a surprisingly clear blue eye at Grant. 'Sly,' he said. 'That's what she be. Sly!'

Rodgers had said, when first he had talked to him, that it was no use dragging below Salcott St Mary, and he had accepted the local man's verdict without asking for an explanation. Now here was Race Memory offering him the explanation.

'Not much use you draggin' anyway,' said Race Memory, wiping the drop from its nose with a gesture that was subtly contemptuous.

'Why? Don't you believe there is a body there?'

'Oh, ah! Body there all right. But that mud there, it don't give up nothin' 'cept in its own time.'

'And when is that likely to be, would you say?'

'Oh! Any time 'tween a thousand years and tomorrow.

Powerful sticky that mud be. Quicksand mud. When my great-grandfer were a little boy he had a barra run down the bank, like, into the water. Quite shallow it were there. He could see the barra but he were frightened, see, to wade in for it. So he run to the cottage. No more'n a few yards. And brung his father out to reach the barra for him. But the mud had it. Ah. The mud had it in the time you'd turn yer back. Not a blink of the barra left. Not even when they got a rake and dragged for it. The mud had it, see. Cannibal mud, that is, I tell ee, cannibal mud.'

'But you say it does give up its victims sometimes.'

'Oh. Ah. Happen.'

'When? In flood?'

'Nah! In flood she just spread herself. Go broody and drop more mud'n ever. Nah. But sometime she be taken aback. Then she let go in surprise.'

'Taken aback?'

'Ah. Same as she were a week since. Cloud come and hit the high country above Otley and burst there, and pour water into the river like someone pouring bath-water away. She have no time to spread out decent and quiet. The water come down channel like a scouring brush and churn her up. Then happen sometimes she loose something from the mud.'

It was a poor outlook, Grant felt, if he had to wait until the next cloudburst to recover Searle's body. The gathering greyness of the day depressed him; in a couple of hours they would have to call it off. By that time, moreover, they would have reached Salcott, and if they had found nothing, what hope was there? He had had a horrible feeling all day that they were merely scratching the surface of that 'immemorial mud'. If this second dragging proved useless, what then? No inquest. No case. No nothing.

By the time a watery sunset was bathing the scene in pallid light they were within fifty yards of the end of their beat. And at that moment Rodgers reappeared and produced an envelope from the pocket of his coat.

'This came for you when I was at the station. It's the report from the States.'

There was no urgency about it now, but he opened it and read it through.

The San Francisco police had no record·against Leslie Searle, and knew of none. He was in the habit of coming to the Coast for the winter months. For the rest of the year he travelled and photographed abroad. He lived well but very quietly, and there was no record of expensive parties or other extravagances of conduct. He had no wife with him and no history of emotional entanglements. The San Francisco police had no record of his origins but they had applied to the Publicity department at Grand Continental, for which studio Searle had photographed Lotta Marlow and Danny Minsky, the reigning stars of the moment. According to Grand Continental, Searle had been born in Jobling, Conn. Only child of Durfey Searle and Christina Mattson. Police at Jobling, Conn., asked about the Searles, said they left town more than twenty years ago and went South somewhere. Searle was a chemist, with a passion for photography, but that is all anyone remembered about them.

Well, it was a dull enough report. An uninspiring collection of unhelpful facts. No clue to the thing he had wanted most; Searle's intimates in the States. No illumination on Searle himself. But something in the report rang a bell in his head.

He read it over again, waiting for that warning click in his mind that was like the sound a clock makes when it is preparing to strike. But this time there was no reaction.

Puzzled, he read it through again, slowly. What was it that had made that warning sound in his mind? He could find nothing. Still puzzled, he folded up the paper and put it away in his pocket.

'We're finished, I suppose you know?' Rodgers said. 'We'll find nothing now. Nothing has ever been taken back from the river at Salcott. In this part of the country they have a proverb. When they want to say: Give a thing up, or: Put it out of your mind for good, they say: "Throw it over the bridge at Salcott".'

'Why don't they dredge the channel instead of letting all this stuff silt up on them,' Grant said, out of temper. 'If they did they wouldn't have the river flooding their houses every second winter.'

Rodgers's long face shortened into amusement and kindliness. 'If you'd ever smelt a bucket of Rushmere mud, you'd think a long time before you'd willingly arrange for it to be dragged up in wagon loads and carted through the street. Shall I stop them now?'

'No,' said Grant, mulishly. 'Let them go on dragging as long as the light lasts. Who knows, we may make history and be the first to take something back from the river at Salcott. I never did believe in those country superstitions, anyhow.'

They did go on dragging till the light went, but the river gave nothing back.

16

'SHALL I give you a lift back to Wickham,' Rodgers asked Grant, but Grant said no, that he had his own car up at the Mill House and would walk up and fetch it.

Marta came out into the windy twilight to meet him, and put her arm through his.

'No?' she said.

'No.'

'Come in and get warm.'

She walked beside him in silence into the house and poured him an out-size whisky. The thick walls shut out the sound of the wind, and the room was quiet and warm as it had been last night. A faint smell of curry came up from the kitchen.

'Do you smell what I am cooking for you?'

'Curry. But you can't be expected to feed the Department.'

'Curry is what you need after a whole day of our English spring glories. You can, of course, go back to the White Hart and have the usual Sunday evening supper of cold tinned beef, two slices of tomato, three cubes of beetroot, and a wilting lettuce leaf.'

Grant shivered unaffectedly. The thought of the White Hart on a Sunday evening was death.

'Besides, tomorrow I shan't be here to give you dinner. I am going back to town. I can't stand the Mill House any more at the moment. I'll stay in town till *Faint Heart* goes into rehearsal.'

'Having you here has practically saved my life,' Grant said. He pulled the American report from his pocket and said: 'Read that, would you, and tell me if anything rings a bell for you.'

'No,' she said, having read. 'No bells. Should it?'

'I don't know. It seemed to me when I read it first that it rang a bell in my mind.' He puzzled over it again for a moment and then put it away.

'When we are both back in town,' Marta said, 'I want to be introduced to your Sergeant Williams. Perhaps you would bring him to dinner one night?'

'But of course,' Grant said, pleased and amused. 'Why this sudden passion for the unknown Williams?'

'Well, I have actually two different reasons. The first is that anyone who has the mother-wit to see that Walter Whitmore is a "push-ee" is worth meeting. And the second is that the only time I have seen you look happy today was after talking to Sergeant Williams on the telephone.'

'Oh, that!' he said; and told her about Benny Skoll, and the *Watchman*, and Williams rebuking virtue. And so they were gay after all over their Sunday supper, with Marta supplying libellous stories of the *Watchman's* theatre critic. So that it was not until he was going that she asked what he was going to do now that the search for Searle had failed.

'I tidy up some ends here in Salcott tomorrow morning,' he said, 'and then I go back to London to report to my chief.'

'And what happens then?'

'There is a conference to decide what action, if any, is to be taken.'

'I understand. Well, when you have got things straightened out ring me up and tell me, won't you. And then we can arrange a night when Sergeant Williams is free.'

How admirable, he thought as he drove away; how truly admirable. No questions, no hints, no little feminine probings. In her acceptance of a situation she was extraordinarily masculine. Perhaps it was this lack of dependence that men found intimidating.

He went back to the White Hart, called the police station to know if there were any messages, picked the menu off the dining-room sideboard to verify Marta's prognostication as to supper (she had forgotten the stewed rhubarb and custard, he must tell her) and for the last time went to bed in the little room under the roof. The text was no promise tonight. THE HOUR COMETH, indeed. What a lot of leisure women seemed to have had once. Now they had everything in cans and had no leisure at all.

But no, it wasn't that, of course. It was that they didn't spend their leisure making texts in coloured wools any more. They went to see Danny Minsky and laughed themselves sick for one-and-tuppence, and if you asked him it was a better way of recovering from the day's work than making meaningless patterns in purple cross-stitch. He glared at the text, tilted the lamp until the shadow blotted out his vision of it, and took his notebooks to bed with him.

In the morning he paid his bill, and pretended not to see the landlord's surprise. Everyone knew that the river-dragging had been unsuccessful, and everyone knew that a piece of clothing recovered from the river had caused that dragging (there were various accounts of which particular piece of clothing), so the landlord hardly expected Scotland Yard to be taking its departure at this juncture. Unless there was a clue that no one knew about?

'Coming back, sir?'

'Not immediately,' Grant said, reading his mind like a book and not particularly liking the stigma of failure that was being tacked on to his name at this moment.

And he headed for Trimmings.

The morning had an air of bland apology. It was smiling wetly and the wind had died. The leaves glittered and the roads steamed in the sun. 'Just my fun, dears,' the English spring was saying to the soaked and shivering mortals who had trusted her.

As the car purred along the slope, towards Trimmings, he looked down at Salcott St Mary in the valley, and thought how odd it was that three days ago it was just a name that Marta used occasionally in conversation. Now it was part of his mind.

And God send it wasn't going to be a burr stuck there for good!

At Trimmings he was received by the refayned Edith, who broke down enough to look humanly scared for a moment when she saw him, and asked to see Walter. She showed him into the fireless library; from which Walter rescued him.

'Come into the drawing-room,' he said. 'We use it as a living-room and there is a fire there'; and Grant caught himself wondering ungratefully whether it was his own comfort that Walter was considering or his guest's. Walter did affect one that way, he observed.

'I am going back to town this morning,' Grant said, 'and there are one or two small points I want to clear up before I make my report to my superiors.'

'Yes?' Walter was nervous and looked as if he had not slept.

'When I asked you about your journey down the Rushmere, you said that you had picked up mail at arranged post-offices.'

'Yes.'

'On Monday there would have been nothing to pick up, but on Tuesday and Wednesday you presumably picked up what there was. Did Searle have any letters on either of those two days, can you remember?'

'There's no difficulty in remembering, Inspector. Searle *never* had *any* mail.'

'Never? You mean Searle had no letters at all while he was at Trimmings?'

'None that I ever knew about. But Liz would tell you. She deals with the post when it comes in.'

How had he missed this small item of information, he wondered.

'Not even forwarded from his hotel or bank?'

'Not that I know of. He may have been letting it mount up. Some people are constitutionally indifferent to letters.'

That was true; and Grant left it there.

'Then about this daily telephoning,' he said. 'You telephoned from Tunstall on Sunday night, from Capel on Monday night, from Friday Street on Tuesday, and from where on Wednesday?'

'There's a call-box at Pett's Hatch. We had meant to camp actually at Pett's Hatch, but that ruined mill looked dreary somehow, and I remembered the sheltered bit farther on where the river turns south, so we went on to there.'

'And you told Trimmings about this proposed camp.'

'Yes, I told you already that we did.'

'I know you did. I don't mean to badger you. What I want to know now is who talked to whom during that call from Pett's Hatch?'

Walter thought for a moment. 'Well, I talked to Miss Fitch first because she was always waiting for the call, then Searle talked to her. Then Aunt Em came—Mrs Garrowby—and talked to Searle for a little and then I finished up by talking to Mrs Garrowby myself. Liz hadn't come in from an errand in the village, so neither of us talked to her on Wednesday.'

'I see. Thank you.' Grant waited, and then said: 'I suppose you don't feel able yet to tell me what the subject of your—disagreement was on Wednesday night?' And as Walter hesitated: 'Is it because it was about Miss Garrowby that you are reluctant to discuss it?'

'I don't want her dragged into this,' Walter said, and Grant could not help feeling that this cliché was less the result of emotion than of a conviction that it was thus an Englishman behaved in the circumstances.

'I ask, as I said before, more as a way of obtaining enlightenment on the subject of Leslie Searle than of pinning you down to anything. Was there anything in that conversation, apart from Miss Garrowby's entry into it, that you would rather I didn't know?'

'No, of course not. It was just about Liz—about Miss Garrowby. It was an extremely silly conversation.'

Grant smiled heartlessly. 'Mr Whitmore, a policeman has experienced the absolute in silliness before he has finished his third year in the force. If you are merely reluctant to put silliness on record, take heart. To me it will probably sound like something near wisdom.'

'There was no wisdom about it. Searle had been in a very odd mood all the evening.'

'Odd? Depressed?' Surely, thought Grant, we aren't going to have to consider suicide at this late stage.

'No. He seemed to be invaded by an unwonted levity. And on the way from the river he began to twit me about —well, about my not being good enough for Liz. For my fiancée. I tried to change the subject, but he kept at it. Until I grew annoyed. He began enumerating all the things he knew about her that I didn't. He would trot out something and say: "I bet you didn't know that about her." '

'Nice things?'

'Oh, yes,' Walter said instantly. 'Yes, of course. Charming things. But it was all so needless and so provocative.'

'Did he suggest that he would be more appreciative in your place?'

'He did more. He said quite frankly that if he put his mind to it he could cut me out. He could cut me out in a fortnight, he said.'

'He didn't offer to bet on it, I suppose?' Grant couldn't help asking.

'No,' Walter said, looking a little surprised.

Grant thought that some day he must tell Marta that she had slipped up in one particular.

'It was when he said that,' Walter said, 'about cutting me out, that I felt I couldn't stand him any more that night. It wasn't the suggestion of my not being his equal that I resented, I hope you understand, Inspector; it was the implied reflection on Liz. On Miss Garrowby. The implication that she would succumb to anyone who used his charms on her.'

'I understand,' said Grant gravely. 'Thank you very much for telling me. Do you think, then, that Searle was deliberately provoking a quarrel?'

'I hadn't thought of it. I just thought he was in a provocative mood. That he was a little above himself.'

'I see. Thank you. Could I speak to Miss Fitch for just one moment. I won't keep her.'

Walter took him to the morning-room where Miss Fitch, with a yellow and a red pencil stuck in her ginger bird's-nest and another in her mouth, was prowling up and down like an enraged kitten. She relaxed when she saw Grant, and looked tired and a little sad.

'Have you come with news, Inspector?' she asked, and Grant, looking past her, saw the fright in Liz's eyes.

'No, I've come to ask you one question, Miss Fitch, and then I shan't bother you again. I apologise for bothering you as it is. On Wednesday night you were waiting for the evening call from your nephew with an account of their progress.'

'Yes.'

'So that you talked to him first. I mean first of the people at Trimmings. Will you go on from there?'

'Tell you what we talked about, you mean?'

'No; who talked to whom.'

'Oh. Well, they were at Pett's Hatch—I suppose you know—and I talked to Walter and then to Leslie. They were both very happy.'

Her voice wavered. 'Then I called Emma—my sister—and she spoke to them both.'

'Did you wait while she spoke to them?'

'No, I went up to my room to see Susie Sclanders's imitations. She does ten minutes on a Wednesday once a month, and she is wonderful, and of course I couldn't listen to her properly with Em talking.'

'I see. And Miss Garrowby?'

'Liz arrived back from the village just too late to talk to them.'

'What time was this, do you remember?'

'I don't remember the exact time, but it must have been about twenty minutes before dinner. We had dinner early that night because my sister was going out to a W.R.I. meeting. Dinner at Trimmings is always being put either back or forwards because someone is either going somewhere or coming from some place.'

'Thank you very much, Miss Fitch. And now, if I might see Searle's room once more I won't bother you again.'

'Yes, of course.'

'I'll take the Inspector up,' Liz said, ignoring the fact that Walter, who was still hovering, was the normal person to escort him.

She got up from the typewriter before Miss Fitch could intervene with any alternative proposal, and led the Inspector out.

'Are you going away because you have come to a

conclusion, Inspector, or because you haven't; or shouldn't I ask that?' she said as they went upstairs.

'I am going as a matter of routine. To do what every officer is expected to do; to present his report to his seniors and let them decide what the facts add up to.'

'But you do some adding first, surely.'

'A lot of subtraction, too,' he said, dryly.

The dryness was not lost on her. 'Nothing makes sense in this case, does it,' she agreed. 'Walter says he couldn't have fallen into the river accidentally. And yet he did fall in. Somehow.'

She paused on the landing outside the tower room. There was a roof-light there and her face was clear in every detail as she turned to him and said: 'The one certain thing in this mess is that Walter had nothing to do with Leslie's death. Please believe that, Inspector. I'm not defending Walter because he is Walter and I am going to marry him. I've known him all my life, and I know what he is capable of and what he is not capable of. And he is not capable of using physical violence to anyone. Do please believe me. He—he just hasn't the *guts*.'

Even his future wife thought him a pushee, Grant observed.

'Don't be misled by that glove, either, Inspector. Do please believe that the most probable explanation is that Leslie picked it up and put it into his pocket meaning to give it back to me. I have looked for the other one of the pair in the car pocket and it isn't there, so the most likely explanation is that they fell out, and Leslie found one and picked it up.'

'Why didn't he put it back in the car pocket?'

'I don't know. Why does one do anything? Putting

something in one's pocket is almost a reflex. The point is that he wouldn't have kept it for the sake of keeping it. Leslie didn't feel about me like that at all.'

The point, Grant thought to himself, wasn't whether Leslie was in love with Liz, but whether Walter believed Liz to be in love with Leslie.

He longed to ask Liz what happens to a girl when she is engaged to a pushee and along comes a left-over from Eden, an escapee from Atlantis, a demon in plain clothes. But the question, though pertinent, would certainly be unproductive. Instead, he asked her if Searle had ever received letters during his stay at Trimmings and she said that as far as she knew he had had none. Then she went away downstairs, and he went into the tower room. The tidy room where Searle had left everything except his personality.

He had not seen it in daylight before, and he spent a few moments having a look at the garden and the valley from the three huge windows. There was one advantage in not caring what your house looked like when it was finished; you could have your windows where they were likely to do most good. Then he turned once more to the task of going through Searle's belongings. Patiently, garment by garment, article by article, he went through them, vainly hoping for some sign, some revelation. He sat in a low chair with the photographic box open on the floor between his feet, and accounted for everything that a photographer might conceivably use. He could think of nothing—neither chemical nor gadget—that was missing from the collection. The box had not been moved since last he saw it, and the empty space still held the outline of what had been abstracted.

It was an innocent space. Articles are abstracted every day from packed cases, leaving the outline of their presence. There was no reason whatever to suppose that what had been taken out was of any significance. But why, in heaven's name, couldn't anyone suggest what that thing might have been?

Once more he tried the small cameras in the space, knowing quite well that they would not fit. He even clapped a pair of Searle's shoes together and tried to fit them into the space. They were half an inch too long and the soles protruded above the general level so that the tray would not fit home and the lid was prevented from shutting. Anyhow, why carry clothing in a photographic box when you had ample room in the appropriate cases? Whatever had occupied the space had not been put in at random or in haste. It had been a neat and methodical packing.

Which suggested that the thing was put there because only Searle himself would have the unpacking of it.

Well, this, in the elegant phrase, was where he got off.

He put everything neatly back as he had found it; took another look at the Rushmere valley, and decided that he had had enough of it; and closed the door on the room where Leslie Searle had left everything but his personality.

17

It was grey in town, but it was a friendly grey and comforting after the rainy levels of the Rushmere. And the young green of the trees in Westminster was vivid as fire against the dark background. It was nice to be among his own kind again; to get into that mental undress that one wears among one's colleagues; to talk the allusive unexplanatory talk that constituted Headquarters' 'shop'.

But it was not so nice to think of the coming interview with Bryce. Would it be one of Bryce's good days or one of his 'off' ones? The Superintendent's average was one off day to three good ones, so the odds were three to one in his favour. On the other hand it was damp weather and the Superintendent's rheumatism was always worst in damp weather.

Bryce was smoking a pipe. So it was one of his good days. (On his off days he lit cigarettes and extinguished them in the ashtray five seconds after he had extinguished the match.)

Grant wondered how to begin. He couldn't very well say: Four days ago you handed over a situation to me, and the situation as far as I'm concerned is in all essentials exactly what it was four days ago. But that, put brutally, was how the case stood.

It was Bryce who saved him. Bryce examined him with his small shrewd eyes, and said: 'If ever I saw

"Please, sir, it wasn't me" written on a man's face, it is on yours now,' and Grant laughed.

'Yes, sir. It's a mess.' He laid his notebooks on the table and took the chair at the other side of the table that was known in the office as the Suspect's Seat.

'You don't think that Bunny-Boy Whitmore did it, then?'

'No, sir. I think it's unlikely to the point of absurdity.'

'Accident?'

'Bunny-Boy doesn't think so,' Grant said with a grin.

'*Doesn't* he, indeed. Hasn't he even enough sense to come in out of the rain?'

'He's a simple sort of creature, in some ways. He just doesn't believe that it was accident, and says so. The fact that it would be to his advantage to have it proved an accident is irrelevant in his view, apparently. He is wildly puzzled and troubled about the disappearance. I am quite sure he had nothing to do with it.'

'Any alternative suggestion?'

'Well, there is someone who had the opportunity, the motive, and the means.'

'What are we waiting for?' Bryce said, flippant.

'Unfortunately the fourth ingredient is missing.'

'No evidence.'

'Not one sliver of a tittle.'

'Who is it?'

'The mother of Walter Whitmore's fiancée. Step-mother actually. She brought Liz Garrowby up from babyhood and is fanatically maternal about her. I don't mean possessive, but——'

'All the best for our Liz.'

'Yes. She was enormously pleased about her step-daughter marrying her nephew, and keeping everything

214

in the family, and I think Searle looked like upsetting the apple-cart. That is a possible motive. She has no alibi for the night in question, and she could have reached the place where they were camped quite easily. She knew where it was because each evening the men telephoned Trimmings, the Fitch place, to report progress, and on Wednesday night they described the place where they were going to bivouac.'

'But she couldn't know that the men would quarrel and go back to the river separately. How was she going to work it?'

'Well, there's an odd thing about that quarrel. Searle from all accounts was a markedly equable person, but it was he who provoked that quarrel. At least Whitmore says so, and I have no reason to doubt him. He twitted Whitmore about not being good enough for Liz Garrowby and boasted that he could take her from him in a week. He was quite sober, so anything so completely out of character must have had an ulterior motive.'

'You think he manufactured a parting with Searle that evening? Why?'

'It *could* have been because he hoped to meet Liz Garrowby somewhere. The Garrowby girl was not at home that evening when the two men telephoned, so Mrs Garrowby did proxy. I suggest that she might also have done proxy in a more serious way.'

' "Liz says will you meet her at the third oak past the old mill".'

'Something like that.'

'And then raging mother waits for him with a blunt instrument and tips the body into the river. I wish to heaven you had been able to recover that body.'

'You don't wish it as badly as I do, sir. Without a corpse where are we?'

'Even with a corpse you have no case.'

'No. But it would be comforting, not to say illuminating, to know the state of the skull bones.'

'Any evidence that Searle was interested in the girl?'

'He had one of her gloves in his collar drawer.'

Bryce grunted. 'I thought that sort of thing went out with valentines,' he said, unconsciously paraphrasing Sergeant Williams.

'I showed it to her and she took it well. Said that he had probably picked it up and meant to give it back to her.'

'And now I'll tell one,' commented the Superintendent.

'She's a nice girl,' Grant said, mildly.

'So was Madeleine Smith. Any second favourite in the suspect stakes?'

'No. Just the field. The men who had no reason to love Searle, and had the opportunity and no satisfactory alibi.'

'Are there many?' Bryce said, surprised by the plural.

'There's Toby Tullis, who is still sick at the snubbing Searle administered. Tullis lives on the river-bank and has a boat. His alibi depends on the word of an infatuated follower. There's Serge Ratoff the dancer, who loathed Searle because of the attention Toby paid him. Serge, according to himself, was dancing on the greensward by the river's rim on Wednesday night. There's Silas Weekley, the distinguished English novelist, who lives in the lane down which Searle disappeared from human ken on Wednesday night. Silas has a thing about beauty; has a constant urge to destroy it. He was working in a hut at the end of the garden that night, so he says.'

'No bets on the field?'

216

'N-o. I think not. A saver on Weekley, perhaps. He is the type that might go over the borderline any day, and spend the rest of his life happily typing away in Broadmoor. But Tullis wouldn't jeopardise all he has built up by a silly murder like this. He is much too shrewd. As for Ratoff, I can imagine him setting off to do a murder, but long before he was half-way there he would have another fine idea and forget what he originally set out to do.'

'Is this village entirely inhabited by crack-pots?'

'It has been "discovered", unfortunately. The aborigines are sane enough.'

'Well, I suppose there is nothing we can do until the body turns up.'

'*If* it turns up.'

'They usually do, in time.'

'According to the local police, five people have been drowned in the Rushmere in the last forty years. That is, leaving Mere Harbour and the shipping part out of the reckoning. Two were drowned higher up than Salcott and three lower down. The three who were drowned lower down than Salcott all turned up within a day or two. The two who were drowned above the village have never turned up at all.'

'It's a nice look-out for Walter Whitmore,' Bryce commented.

'Yes,' Grant said, thinking it over. 'They weren't very kind to him this morning.'

'The papers? No. Awfully good-mannered and discreet but they couldn't have made pleasant reading for Bunny-Boy. A nasty spot to be in. No accusation, so no possible defence. Not that he *has* any,' he added.

He was silent for a little, tapping his teeth with his pipe as was his habit when cogitating.

'Well, I suppose there is nothing we can do at the moment. You make a neat shipshape report and we'll see what the Commissioner says. But I don't see that there is anything more we can do. Death by drowning, no evidence so far to show whether accidental or otherwise. That's your conclusion, isn't it?'

As Grant did not answer immediately, he looked up and said sharply: 'Isn't it?'

Now you see it, now you don't.

Something wrong in the set-up.

Don't let your flair ride you, Grant.

Something phoney somewhere.

Now you see it, now you don't.

Conjurer's patter.

The trick of the distracted attention.

You could get away with anything if you distracted the attention.

Something phoney somewhere. . . .

'Grant!'

He came back to the realisation of his chief's surprise. What was he to say? Acquiesce and let it go? Stick to the facts and the evidence, and stay on the safe side?

With a detached regret he heard his own voice saying: 'Have you ever seen a lady sawn in half, sir?'

'I have,' Bryce said, eyeing him with a wary disapproval.

'It seems to me that there is a strong aroma of sawn-lady about this case,' Grant said; and then remembered that this was the metaphor he had used to Sergeant Williams.

But Bryce's reaction was very different from the Sergeant's.

'Oh, my *God*!' he groaned. 'You're *not* going to do a Lamont on us, are you, Grant?'

Years ago Grant had gone into the farthest Highlands after a man and had brought him back; brought him back sewn up in a case so fault-proof that only the sentence remained to be said; and had handed him over with the remark that on the whole he thought they had got the wrong man. (They had.) The Yard had never forgotten it, and any wild opinion in contradiction to the evidence was still known as 'doing a Lamont'.

The sudden mention of Jerry Lamont heartened Grant. It had been even more absurd to feel that Jerry Lamont was innocent, in the face of an unbreakable case, than it was to smell 'sawn-lady' in a simple drowning.

'Grant!'

'There's something very odd about the set-up,' Grant said stubbornly.

'What is odd?'

'If I knew that it would be down in my report. It isn't any one thing. It's the—the whole set-up. The atmosphere. The smell of it. It doesn't smell right.'

'Couldn't you just explain to an ordinary hard-working policeman *what* smells so wrong about it?'

Grant ignored the Superintendent's heavy-handedness, and said:

'It's all wrong from the beginning, don't you see. Searle's walking in from nowhere, into the party. Yes, I know that we know about him. That he is who he says he is, and all that. We even know that he came to England just as he says he did. Via Paris. His place was booked by the American Express office at the Madeleine. But that doesn't alter the fact that the whole episode has something queer about it. *Was* it so likely that he would be all that keen to meet Walter just because they were both friends of Cooney Wiggin?'

'Don't ask me! Was it?'

'Why this need to meet Walter?'

'Perhaps he had seen him broadcast and just couldn't wait.'

'And he had no letters.'

'Who hadn't?'

'Searle. He had no letters all the time he was at Salcott.'

'Perhaps he is allergic to the gum on envelopes. Or I *have* heard that people leave letters lying at their bank to be called for.'

'That's another thing. None of the usual American banks or agencies has ever heard of him. And there is one tiny thing that seems odd to me out of all proportion to its actual value. Actual value to this case, I mean. He had a tin box, rather like an outsize paint-box, that he used to hold all his photographic stuff. Something is gone out of the box. Something roughly 9 inches by $3\frac{1}{2}$ by 4, that was packed in the lower compartment (it has a tray like a paint-box with a deeper space below). Nothing that is now among his belongings fits the space, and no one can suggest what the thing could have been.'

'And what is so odd about that? There must be a hundred and one things that might have been packed in a space that size.'

'As what, for instance, sir?'

'Well—well, I can't think off-hand, but there must be dozens.'

'There is ample space in his other cases for anything he wanted to pack. So it wouldn't be clothes, or ordinary possessions. Whatever was there, in the tin box, was something that he kept where only he would be likely to handle it.'

Bryce's attention grew more sober at that.

'Now it is missing. It is of no obvious importance in this case. No importance at all, perhaps. It is just an oddity and it sticks in my mind.'

'What do you think he might have been after at Trimmings? Blackmail?' Bryce asked, with interest at last.

'I don't know. I hadn't thought of blackmail.'

'What could have been in the box that he could turn into cash? Not letters, that shape. Documents, perhaps? Documents in a roll.'

'I don't know. Yes, perhaps. The thing against the blackmail idea is that he seemed to have ample means.'

'Blackmailers usually have.'

'Yes. But Searle had a profession that kept him very nicely. Only a hog would want more. And somehow he didn't look to me like a hog.'

'Be your age, Grant. Just sit quiet for a moment and think of the blackmailers you have known.' He watched this shot go home, and said, dryly: 'Exactly!' And then: 'Who would you say was the blackmailee at Trimmings? Mrs Garrowby got a past, do you think?'

'Possibly,' Grant said, considering Emma Garrowby in a new light. 'Yes, I think it's quite possible.'

'Well, the choice isn't very wide. I don't suppose Lavinia Fitch was ever out on the tiles?'

Grant thought of kind, anxious little Miss Fitch, with the bristling pencils in her mop of hair, and smiled.

'There isn't much choice, you see. I suppose if it was blackmail at all it must have been Mrs Garrowby. So your theory is that Searle was murdered for a reason that has nothing to do with Liz Garrowby.' And as Grant made no immediate answer to that, 'You believe that it *was* murder, don't you.'

'No.'

'No!'

'I don't believe he's dead.'

There was a moment of silence. Then Bryce leaned forward over the table and said with immense self-control: 'Now, look here, Grant. Flair's flair. And you're entitled to your whack of it. But when you take to throwing it about in chunks it becomes too much of a good thing. Have a little moderation, for Pete's sake. You've been dragging a river for a whole day yesterday trying to find a drowned man, and now you have the nerve to sit there and tell me you don't think he was drowned at all. What do you think he did? Walked away barefoot? Or hobbled away disguised as a one-legged man supported by crutches which he had tossed off in an idle moment from a couple of oak branches? Where do you think he went to? What is he going to live on from now on? Honestly, Grant, I think you must need a holiday. What, just tell me *what*, put this notion into your head? *How* does a trained detective mind jump from a straightforward case of "missing believed drowned" into a wild piece of fantasy that has no connection with anything in the case at all?'

Grant was silent.

'Come on, Grant. I'm not ribbing you. I really want to know. How do you arrive at the conclusion that a man isn't drowned after finding his shoe in the river? How did the shoe get there?'

'If I knew that, sir, I'd have my case.'

'Did Searle have a spare pair of shoes with him?'

'No. Just the ones he was wearing.'

'The one that was found in the river.'

'Yes, sir.'

'And you still think he didn't drown?'

'Yes.'

There was a silence.

'I don't know which to admire more, Grant: your nerve or your imagination.'

Grant said nothing. There seemed to be nothing to say. He was bitterly aware that he had already said too much.

'Can you think of any theory, however wild, that would fit your idea of his being alive?'

'I can think of one. He could have been abducted, and the shoe tossed in the river as evidence of drowning.'

Bryce regarded him with dramatised respect. 'You mistook your vocation, Grant. You're a very good detective, but as a writer of detective fiction you'd make a fortune.'

'I was only answering your challenge and supplying a theory to fit the facts, sir,' Grant said mildly. 'I didn't say I believed in it.'

This slowed Bryce down a little. 'Take them out of a hat like rabbits, do you. Theories in all sizes to fit any figure! No compulsion to buy! Walk up! Walk up!' He stopped and looked for a long moment at Grant's imperturbable face, sat slowly back in his chair, relaxed, and smiled. 'You damned poker-face, you!' he said amiably. He searched in his pocket for matches. 'Do you know what I envy about you, Grant? Your self-control. I'm always flying off the handle about something or other; and it doesn't do me or anyone else any good. My wife says that it is because I'm not sure of myself and I'm afraid I'm not going to get my way. She attended a course of six lectures on psychology at Morley College, and there is nothing about the human mind she doesn't know. I can only conclude that you must be damned sure of yourself behind that nice equable temper of yours.'

'I don't know, sir,' Grant said, amused. 'I was anything but equable when I came in to report, and had nothing to show you but a situation that was exactly the same as it was when you handed it over to me four days ago.'

'So you said: "How's the old man's rheumatism today? Is he approachable or do I go on all fours?" ' His little elephant eyes twinkled for a moment. 'Well, I suppose we present the Commissioner with your neat report of the facts as they exist, and leave him in ignorance of the finer flights of your imagination.'

'Oh, yes, sir. I can't very well explain to the Commissioner that I have a feeling in the pit of my stomach.'

'No. And if you'll take my advice, you'll stop paying so much attention to the rumblings of your stomach, and stick to what goes on in your head. There is a little phrase commonly used in police work that says, "in accordance with the evidence". You say that over six times a day as a grace before and after meals, and perhaps it will keep your feet on the ground and stop you ending up thinking you're Frederick the Great or a hedgehog or something.'

18

In his schooldays Grant had learned that if he was
stumped by a problem it paid to leave it alone for a
while. A proposition that had seemed insoluble the night
before was simple to the point of being obvious in the
light of morning. This was a lesson that he learned for
himself and consequently never forgot, and he took it
with him both into his personal life and into his work.
Whenever he reached deadlock he transferred his
attention. So now, although he did not follow Bryce's
advice about the daily ritual, he did give heed to his
words about ignoring 'the rumblings of his stomach'.
Where the Searle affair was concerned he had reached
deadlock, so he withdrew his attention and thought
upon Tom Thumb. The current Tom Thumb being an
'Arab' potentate who had lived at a Strand hotel for a
fortnight, and had disappeared without the formality of
paying his bill.

The daily routine, a routine where there was always
more work than men to do it, sucked him back into its
vortex, and Salcott St Mary disappeared from the
forefront of his mind.

Then, on a morning six days later, his mind flung it
back at him.

He was walking along the south pavement of the
Strand on his way to lunch in Maiden Lane, pleased

with the report that he was going to give Bryce when he went back to the Yard, and wondering idly at the large display of women's shoes in a street as unpopular with women as the Strand. The thought of women's shoes reminded him of Dora Siggins and the slippers she had bought for the dance, and he smiled a little to himself as he began to cross the street, remembering her vitality and her chatter and her friendly sharpness. She had nearly left the shoes behind after all, he remembered; even after missing a bus home in order to buy them. They had been lying on the seat because they wouldn't fit into her packed shopping bag, and he had had to point them out to her. An untidy parcel in cheap brown paper, with the heels——

He stopped dead.

A taxi driver, his face contorted with rage and fright, yelled something into his ear. Brakes screamed as a lorry came to a halt at his elbow. A policeman, hearing the yelling brakes and the protests, made slow but purposeful movements in his direction. But Grant did not wait. He flung himself against the next approaching taxi, wrenched the door open, and said 'Scotland Yard and quick' to the driver.

'Exhibitionist!' said the driver, and chugged away to the Embankment.

But Grant did not hear him. His mind was busy on the old sucked-dry problem that suddenly seemed so new and exciting now that he had taken it out again. At the Yard he looked for Williams and when he had found him he said: 'Williams, remember saying on the telephone that all your Wickham notes were good for was the wastepaper basket? And I said never to destroy notes.'

'I remember,' Williams said. 'When I was in town picking up Benny Skoll and you were at Salcott dragging the river.'

'You didn't by any chance take my advice, did you?'

'Of course I took your advice, sir. I *always* take your advice.'

'You have those notes somewhere?'

'I have them right here in my desk.'

'May I see them?'

'Certainly, sir. Though I don't know if you can read them.'

It was certainly not easy. When Williams wrote a report it was in a faultless schoolboy script, but when making notes for his own use he indulged in a hieroglyphic shorthand of his own.

Grant flipped over the pages looking for what he wanted.

' "The 9.30 Wickham to Crome",' he murmured. ' "The 10.5 Crome to Wickham. The 10.15 Wickham to Crome." 'M. 'M. "Farm lane: old"——old *what* and child?'

'Old labourer and child. I didn't detail what they had in the buses to start with. Just what they picked up on the road.'

'Yes, yes; I know; I understand. "Long Leat cross-roads." Where is that?'

'It's a "green" place, a sort of common, on the outskirts of Wickham, where there's a collection of Fair stuff. A merry-go-round and things.'

'I remember. "Two roundabout men, known." Is it "known"?'

'Yes; known to the conductor personally from other journeys.'

' "Woman going to Warren Farm, known." What comes after that, Williams?'

Williams translated to him what came after that.

Grant wondered what Williams would think if he flung his arms round him and embraced him, after the fashion of Association Footballers to successful goal shooters.

'May I keep this for the moment?' he asked.

He could keep it for good, Williams said. It wasn't likely to be much good now. Unless—unless, of course——

Grant could see the dawning realisation that this sudden interest in his notes must come from more than academic curiosity on Grant's part; but he did not wait to answer the coming question. He went to see Bryce.

'It's my belief,' Bryce said, glaring at him, 'that the lower ranks in this institution prolong hotel cases so that they can sit in the back room with the manager and be given drinks on the house.'

Grant ignored his libellous pleasantry.

'Is this a routine report before you sit down to a nice leisurely lunch, or have you something to tell me?'

'I think I've got something that will please you, sir.'

'It will have to be very good to please me today, as perhaps you've noticed.'

'I've discovered that he had a passion for cherry brandy.'

'*Very* interesting, I must say. *Fascinatingly* interesting! And what good do you think——' A wonderful thought suddenly brightened the bleak small eye. He looked at Grant, as one colleague to another. '*No!*' he said. '*Not* Hamburg Willy!'

'Looks like it, sir. It has all the earmarks; and he'd make a very good Arab with that Jewish profile of his.'

'Hamburg! Well, well! What did he get out of it that was worth the risk?'

'Soft living for a fortnight; and some fun.'

'It's going to be expensive fun. I suppose you've no idea where he can have skipped to?'

'Well, I remembered that he has been living with Mabs Hankey, and Mabs is doing a turn at the Acacias in Nice this spring; so I spent most of the morning on the telephone and I find that our Willy, or what I take to be our Willy, is staying there as Monsieur Goujon. What I came to ask, sir, was if, now that it is routine, someone else could take over the extradition and all that and leave me free for a day or two to do something else.'

'What do you want to do?'

'I've got a new idea about the Searle case.'

'Now, Grant!' Bryce said, in warning.

'It's too new'—'and too silly,' he added to himself—'to talk about, but I would very much like to spend a little time on it and see if it works out, sir.'

'Well, I suppose, after the cherry brandy, you think I can't very well refuse you.'

'Thank you, sir.'

'But if it doesn't look like panning out, I hope you'll drop it. There's plenty of work right here without you running after rainbows and pots of gold.'

So Grant walked out of the Superintendent's room in pursuit of his pot of gold, and the first thing he did was to go to his own room and take out the report that the San Francisco police had sent them about Searle. He studied it for a long time, and then sent a polite request to the police of Jobling, Conn.

Then he remembered that he had not yet had lunch.

He wanted quiet in which to think, so he put the precious sheet of paper into his wallet and went out to his favourite pub, where the rush would be over and they would manage to scrape up something for him. He still did not know what in that account of Searle's life in America had rung a bell in his mind when he had first read it. But he was beginning to have an idea as to what *kind* of thing it was that had rung that bell.

As he was walking out of the pub after lunch he knew what it might have been.

He went back to the Yard and consulted a reference book.

Yes, it was that.

He took out the San Francisco report and compared it with the entry in the reference book.

He was jubilant.

He had the important thing. The thing he needed to stand on. He had the connection between Searle and Walter Whitmore.

He rang up Marta Hallard, and was told that she was rehearsing for *Faint Heart*. She would be at the Criterion this afternoon.

Feeling ridiculously like a bubble—so help me, you could bounce me like a ball, he thought—he floated up to Piccadilly Circus. I feel just the way Tommy Thrupp looked last Sunday morning, he thought. Twice as large as life, with lightning shooting out of my head like toasting-forks.

But the Criterion in the throes of a rehearsal afternoon soon reduced him to life-size and brought his feet back on to the ground.

He walked in through the foyer, stepped over the

symbolical barrier of a draped cord, and went down the stairs into the earth without interference from anyone. Perhaps they think I look like an author, he thought, and wondered who had written *Faint Heart*. No one ever did know who had written a play. Playwrights must lead blighted lives. Fifty to one, on an actuary's reckoning, against their play running more than three weeks; and then no one even noticed their name on the programme.

And something like a thousand to one against any play ever getting as far as rehearsals even. He wondered whether the author of *Faint Heart* was aware that he was one in a thousand, or whether he was just sure of it.

Somewhere in the bowels of the earth he came on the elegant little box that was the Criterion's auditorium; a little ghostly in the cold light of unshaded electrics, but reticent and well-bred. Various dim shapes lay about in the stalls, and no one made any move to ask his business.

Marta, alone on the stage with a horse-hair sofa and a scared-looking young man, was saying: 'But I *must* lie on the sofa, Bobby darling. It's a waste of my legs if I just sit. Everyone looks the same from the knees down.'

'Yes, Marta, you are right, of course,' said Bobby, who was the dim figure prowling up and down in front of the orchestra pit.

'I don't want to alter your conception in any way, Bobby, but I do think——'

'Yes, Marta dear, you are right, of course, so right. No, of course it won't make any difference. No, I assure you. It really is all right. It'll look grand.'

'Of course it may be difficult for Nigel——'

'No, Nigel can come round behind you before he says his line. Try it, Nigel, will you.'

Marta draped herself over the horse-hair and the scared-looking boy went away and made his entrance. He made his entrance nine times. 'Well, it's coming,' Bobby said, letting him away with the ninth.

Someone in the stalls went out and came back with cups of tea.

Nigel said his line above the sofa, to the right of the sofa, to the left of the sofa, and without relation to the sofa at all.

Someone came into the stalls and collected the empty cups.

Grant moved over to a lonely lounger and asked: 'When do you think I shall be able to speak to Miss Hallard?'

'*No one* will be able to speak to her if she has much more of Nigel today.'

'I have very important business with her.'

'You the clothes man?'

Grant said that he was a personal friend of Miss Hallard's and must talk to her for a few moments. He wouldn't keep her longer than that.

'Oh.' The dim figure crawled away and consulted with another. It was like some muffled ritual.

The consulted one detached himself from the group of shadows to which he belonged and came over to Grant. He introduced himself as the stage-manager, and asked what exactly it was that Grant wanted. Grant said that at the very first opportunity would someone tell Miss Hallard that Alan Grant was here and wanted to speak to her for a moment.

This worked; and during the next pause, the stage-manager crept on to the stage and bending apologetically over Marta murmured something in a wood-pigeon undertone.

Marta got up from the couch and came down to the edge of the stage, shading her eyes in an effort to see beyond the lights into the dark auditorium.

'Are you there, Alan?' she said. 'Come through the pass door, will you? Show him where it is, someone.'

She came to meet him at the pass door and was plainly glad to see him. 'Come and have a cup of tea in the wings with me while the young lovers get on with it. Thank God that I shall never again have to be one of a pair of young lovers! The theatre's most boring convention. You've never come to rehearsal before, Alan! What moved you to it?'

'I would like to say that it was intellectual curiosity, but I'm afraid it is just business. You can help me, I think.'

She helped him enormously; and never once asked what these questions might mean.

'We haven't had that dinner with your Sergeant Williams,' she said as she went away to make the young lovers look like amateurs and wish that they had gone on the land.

'If you wait for a week or so, Sergeant Williams and I may have a story to tell you.'

'Splendid. I've earned it, I feel. I've been so good and discreet.'

'You've been wonderful,' he said, and went away out the back way into the lane with a slight recurrence of the jubilation that had floated him down the stairs at his entrance.

Armed with the information Marta had given him, he

233

went to Cadogan Gardens and interviewed the house-keeper of some furnished flats.

'Oh, yes, I remember,' she said. 'They ran about a lot together. Oh, no, she didn't stay here. These are bachelor flats; I mean, flats for one. But she was around a lot.'

And by that time London was shutting up shop for the night and there was nothing more he could do until the police of Jobling, Conn., supplied him with the information he had asked for. So he went home early for once, had a light supper, and went to bed. He lay for a long time working it out in his mind. Working out the details. Working out the wherefore.

Toby Tullis had wanted to know what made Leslie Searle tick; and Grant, too, lying with his eyes on the ceiling, unmoving for an hour at a time, was looking for the mainspring of Leslie Searle's mind.

19

It was forty-eight hours before word came from Jobling, Conn., and half a dozen times in those forty-eight hours Grant was on the brink of going to that woman in Hampstead and dragging the truth from her by main force. But he restrained himself. He would deal with her presently. Her lies would be neatly laid out on a plate, and presented to her when the time came.

He would wait for that report.

And the report when it came proved worth waiting for.

Grant read it through in one swift eye movement, and then he sat back and laughed.

'If anyone wants me for the rest of the day,' he said to Sergeant Williams, 'I'll be at Somerset House.'

'Yes, sir,' Williams said, subdued.

Grant glanced at Williams's unwontedly sober features —Williams was a little hurt that Grant was playing a lone hand over this—and was reminded of something.

'By the way, Williams, Miss Hallard is very anxious to meet you. She has asked me if I would bring you to dinner one night.'

'Me?' said Williams going pink. 'What on earth for?'

'She has fallen a victim to your reported charms. She asked me to arrange a night when you were free. I feel in my bones this morning that by Saturday both you and I will be in a state for celebration; and it would be appropriate if we celebrated with Marta, I think. Saturday any good to you?'

'Well, Nora and I usually go to the movies on Saturday, but when I'm on duty she goes with Jen. That's her sister. So I don't see why she shouldn't go with Jen this week.'

'When she hears that you are going to dine with Marta Hallard she'll probably start divorce proceedings.'

'Not her. She'll wait up for me so that she can ask me what Marta Hallard was wearing,' said Williams, the Benedict.

Grant rang to ask Marta if he could bring Sergeant Williams to meet her on Saturday night, and then went away and buried himself in Somerset House.

And that night he did not lie awake. He was like a child that goes to sleep because that way it will quickly be tomorrow. Tomorrow, the one small piece would fall into place and make the pattern whole.

If the one small piece happened not to fit, of course, then the whole picture was wrong. But he was pretty sure that it would fit.

In the short interval between putting out the lamp and falling asleep he ranged sleepily over the 'field'. When that one small piece fell into place tomorrow, life would be a great deal happier for a great many people. For Walter, naturally; Walter would have the shadow of suspicion lifted from him. For Emma Garrowby, with her Liz made safe. For Liz? Relief unspeakable for Liz. And relief for Miss Fitch—who might, he suspected, be a little sad, too. But she could always put it in a book. In a book was where the thing belonged.

Toby would have quite special reasons for self-congratulation, Grant thought; and laughed. And Serge Ratoff would be comforted.

Silas Weekley would not care at all.

He remembered that Marta had remarked on how 'nice' Leslie and Liz had been together. ('A natural pair,' she said—but she could never have guessed *how* natural!) Was it just possible that Liz would be hurt when that one small piece fell into place tomorrow? He hoped not. He liked Liz Garrowby. He would like to think that Searle had meant nothing to her. That she would find nothing but happiness and relief in the vindication of her Walter.

What was it Marta had said? 'I don't think Walter knows anything about Liz, and I have an idea that Leslie Searle knew quite a lot.' (Surprising, how Marta had seen that without any clue to the source of Searle's understanding.) But it did not matter very much, Grant thought, that Walter did not know very much about Liz. Liz, he was quite sure, knew all that was to be known about Walter; and that was a very good basis for a happy married life.

He fell asleep wondering if being married to someone as nice and intelligent and lovable as Liz Garrowby would compensate a man for the loss of his freedom.

A procession of his loves—romantic devotions most of them—trailed away into the distance as his mind blurred into unconsciousness.

But in the morning he had thought for only one woman. That woman in Hampstead.

Never, even at his most callow, had he gone to see any woman with an eagerness as great as the one that was taking him to Holly Pavement this morning. And he was a little shocked as he got off the bus and walked towards the Holly Pavement turning to find that his heart was thumping. It was a very long time indeed since Grant's heart had thumped for any but a purely physical reason.

Damn the woman, he thought, damn the woman.

Holly Pavement was a backwater filled with sunlight; a place so quiet that the strutting pigeons seemed almost rowdy. Number nine was a two-storey house, and the upper storey had been apparently converted into a studio. There were two push-buttons on the bell plaque with neat wooden labels alongside. 'Miss Lee Searle', said the upper one; 'Nat Gansage: Accessories', said the lower.

Wondering what 'accessories' were, Grant pressed the upper button, and presently heard her coming down the wooden stairs to the door. The door opened, and she was standing there.

'Miss Searle?' he heard himself say.

'Yes,' she said, waiting there in the sunlight, unperturbed but puzzled.

'I am Detective-Inspector Grant of the C.I.D.' Her puzzlement deepened at that, he noticed. 'A colleague of mine, Sergeant Williams, came to see you in my stead a week ago because I was otherwise engaged. I would like very much to talk to you myself, if it is convenient.'

And it had better be convenient, blast you, he said in his mind; furious at his racing heart.

'Yes, of course,' she said equably. 'Come in, won't you. I live upstairs.'

She shut the door behind him and then led him up the wooden stairs to her studio. A strong smell of coffee

—good coffee—pervaded the place and as she led him in she said: 'I've just been having my breakfast. I have made a bargain with the paper boy that he should leave a roll for me every morning with the paper, and that is my breakfast. But there is lots of coffee. Will you have some, Inspector?'

They said at the Yard that Grant had two weaknesses: coffee, and coffee. And it smelt wonderful. But he wasn't going to drink anything with Lee Searle.

'Thank you, but I have just had mine.'

She poured another cup for herself, and he noticed that her hand was quite steady. Damn the woman, he was beginning to admire her. As a colleague she would be wonderful.

She was a tall woman, and spare; very good-looking in her bony fashion and still quite young. She wore her hair in a thick plait, coronet-wise. The long housecoat she was wearing was made of some dull green stuff, rather like one Marta had; and she had the long legs that helped to give Marta her elegance.

'Your resemblance to Leslie Searle is remarkable,' he said.

'So we have been told,' she said shortly.

He moved round the room to look at the Scottish pictures that were still propped up on view. They were orthodox impressions of orthodox scenes, but they were painted with a savage confidence, a fury, so that they shouted at one from the canvas. They didn't present themselves to one, they attacked. 'Look, I'm Suilven!' shouted Suilven, looking odder and more individual than even that mountain had ever looked. The Coolin, a grape-blue rampart against a pale morning sky, were a whole barrier of arrogance. Even the calm waters of Kishorn were insolent.

'Did it stay fine for you?' Grant asked, and then, feeling that that was too impudent, added: 'The West of Scotland is very wet.'

'Not at this time of year. This is the best time.'

'Did you find the hotels comfortable? I hear they are apt to be primitive.'

'I didn't trouble the hotels. I camped out in my car.'

Neat, he thought. Very neat.

'What was it you wanted to talk to me about?'

But he was in no hurry. She had caused him a lot of trouble, this woman. He would take his time.

He moved from the pictures to the rows of books on the shelves, and considered the titles.

'You have a liking for oddities, I see.'

'Oddities?'

'Poltergeists. Showers of fish. Stigmata. That sort of thing.'

'I think all artists are attracted by the odd, whatever their medium, don't you?'

'You don't seem to have anything on transvestism.'

'What made you think of that?'

'Then you know the term?'

'Of course.'

'It is something that doesn't interest you?'

'The literature of the subject is very unsatisfactory, I understand. Nothing between learned pamphlets and *News of the World*.'

'You ought to write a treatise on the subject.'

'*I*?'

'You like oddities,' he said smoothly.

'I am a painter, Inspector, not a writer. Besides, no one is interested nowadays in female pirates.'

'Pirates?'

'They were all pirates or soldiers or sailors, weren't they?'

'You think the fashion went out with Phoebe Hessel? Oh, by no means. The thing is continually turning up. Only the other day a woman died in Gloucestershire who had worked for more than twenty years hauling timber and coal, and even the doctor who attended her in her last illness had no idea that she was not a man. I knew a case personally, not long ago. A young man was charged in a London suburb with theft. Quite a normal popular young man. Played a good game of billiards, belonged to a men's club, and was walking out with one of the local beauties. But when medically examined he turned out to be quite a normal young woman. It happens somewhere or other every year or two. Glasgow. Chicago. Dundee. In Dundee a young woman shared a lodging-house ward with ten men and was never questioned. Am I boring you?'

'Not at all. I was only wondering whether you considered them oddities in the sense that stigmata and poltergeists are.'

'No; oh, no. Some, of course, are genuinely happier in men's things; but a great many do it from love of adventure, and a few from economic necessity. And some because it is the only way in which they can work out their schemes.'

She sipped her coffee with polite interest, as one indulging an uninvited guest until he should reach the point of stating what he had come for.

Yes, he thought, she would make a wonderful ally.

His heart had slowed down to its proper rate. These were moves in a game that he had been playing a long time; the game of mind against mind. And now he was interested in her reaction to his moves. She had withstood undermining. How would she stand up to direct attack?

He came away from the bookshelves and said: 'You were very devoted to your cousin, Miss Searle.'

'Leslie? But I have already——'

'No. Marguerite Merriam.'

'Mar——. I don't know what you are talking about.'

That was a mistake. If she had stopped to think for a moment, she would have realised that there was no reason at all to deny the connection with Marguerite. But the unexpectedness of that name on his lips had startled her, and she had fallen headlong.

'So devoted that you couldn't think quite straight about her.'

'I tell you——'

'No, don't tell me anything. I'll tell you something. Something that ought to make confidences between us quite easy, Miss Searle. I encountered Leslie Searle at a party in Bloomsbury. One of those literary gatherings. He wanted to be introduced to Lavinia Fitch and I agreed to present him. As we pushed through the crowd we were flung together at very close quarters; in fact it was breathing-room only. A policeman is trained to observe, but I think even without that I would have noticed any variation in detail that was presented to me at that range. He had very fine grey eyes, Leslie Searle, and there was a small brown fleck in the iris of the left one. I have lately spent a good deal of time, and a great deal of labour and thought, trying to account for Leslie Searle's disappearance, and with native wit and considerable luck I got to the stage where I needed only one small thing to make my case complete. A small brown fleck. I found it on the doorstep down there.'

There was complete silence. She was sitting with her coffee cup in her lap, looking down at it. The slow ticking of a wall clock sounded loud and pónderous in the quiet.

'It's an odd thing, sex,' Grant said. 'When you laughed with me, caught in the crush that day, I had a moment of being suddenly out of countenance. Disconcerted: The way a dog is sometimes when it is laughed at. I knew it had nothing to do with your laughing, and I could not think why else I should have been disconcerted. About 12.45 last Monday I began the process of realising why; and was nearly run over by a taxi in consequence.'

She had looked up at this; and now she said in a kind of detached interest: 'Are you the star turn at Scotland Yard?'

'Oh, no,' Grant assured her. 'I come in bundles.'

'You don't talk like something out of a bundle. Not any bundles I've been acquainted with. And no one out of a bundle could have—could have found out what happened to Leslie Searle.'

'Oh, I'm not responsible for that.'

'No? Who is, then?'

'Dora Siggins.'

'Dora——? Who is she?'

'She left her shoes on the seat of my car. Tied up in a neat parcel. At the time they were just Dora Siggins's shoes tied up in a parcel. But at 12.45 last Monday, right in the path of a taxi, they became a parcel of the required dimensions.'

'What dimensions?'

'The dimensions of that empty space in your photographic box. I did try a pair of Searle's shoes in that space—you must allow me so much—but you'll admit that no run-of-the-mill hard-working one-of-a-bundle detective would think up anything so outré as a parcel containing one pair of women's shoes and a coloured silk head-square. By the way, my sergeant's recorded description of the woman who joined the bus at that cross-roads where the fair is, says: Loose gaberdine raincoat.'

'Yes. My burberry is a reversible one.'

'Was that part of the preparation too?'

'No; I got it years ago, so that I could travel light. I could camp out in it, and go to afternoon tea with the inside out.'

'It is a little galling to think that it was I who paved the way for this practical joke of yours by my anxiety to be helpful to the stranger within the gates. I'll let strangers stand after this.'

'Is that how it seems to you?' she said slowly. 'A practical joke?'

'Let us not quibble about terms. I don't know what you call it to yourself. What it actually is, is a practical joke of particular brutality. I take it that your plan was either to make a fool of Walter Whitmore or to leave him in the soup.'

'Oh, no,' she said simply. 'I was going to kill him.'

Her sincerity was so patent that this brought Grant up all standing.

'Kill him?' he said, all attention and his flippancy gone.

'It seemed to me that he shouldn't be allowed to go on

living,' she said. She took her coffee cup off her lap to put it on the table, but her hand was shaking so much that she could not lift it.

Grant moved over and took it from her, gently, and set it down.

'You hated him because of what you imagined he had done to Marguerite Merriam,' he said, and she nodded. Her hands were clasped in her lap in a vain effort to keep them steady.

He was silent for a moment or two, trying to get used to the idea that all the ingenuity that he had taken to be her slick exit from a masquerade had been in reality a planned get-out to murder.'

'And what made you change your mind?'

'Well—oddly enough, the first small thing was something Walter said. It was one evening after Serge Ratoff had made a scene in the pub.'

'Yes?'

'Walter said that when one was as devoted as Serge was to anyone one ceased to be quite sane about it. That made me think a bit.' She paused. 'And then, I liked Liz. She wasn't at all what I had pictured. You see, I had pictured her as the girl who had stolen Walter from Marguerite. And the real Liz wasn't like that at all. That sort-of bewildered me a little. But the real thing that stopped me was—was that—that——'

'You found out that the person you loved had never existed,' Grant said quietly.

She caught her breath and said: 'I don't know how you could have guessed that.'

'But that is what happened, isn't it?'

'Yes. Yes, I found out—— People didn't know that

245

I had any connection with her, you see, and they talked quite unguardedly. Marta, especially. Marta Hallard. I went back with her one night after dinner. She told me things that—shocked me. I had always known that she was wild and—and headstrong—Marguerite, I mean—but one expects that of genius, and she seemed so —so vulnerable that one forgave——'

'Yes, I understand.'

'But the Marguerite that Marta and those other people knew was someone I didn't know at all. Someone I wouldn't even have liked if——. I remember when I said that at least she *lived*, Marta said: "The trouble was that she didn't allow anyone else to. The suction she created" Marta said "was so great that her neighbours were left in a vacuum. They either expired from suffocation or they were dashed to death against the nearest large object." So you see, I didn't feel like killing Walter any more. But I still hated him for leaving her. I couldn't forget that. That he had walked out on her and she had killed herself because of it. Oh, I know, I know!' she added, as she saw his interruption coming. 'It was not that she loved him so much. I know that now. But if he had stayed with her she would be alive today, alive, with her genius and her beauty and her gay loveliness. He might have waited——'

'Till she tired?' Grant supplied, more dryly than he had intended, and she winced.

'It wouldn't have been long,' she said, with sad honesty.

'May I change my mind and have some of that coffee after all?' Grant said.

She looked at her uncontrolled hands and said: 'Will you pour it out?'

She watched him as he poured, and said: 'You are a very strange policeman.'

'As I said to Liz Garrowby when she made the same remark: It may be your idea of policemen that's strange.'

'If I had had a sister like Liz how different my life would have been. I had no one but Marguerite. And when I heard that she had killed herself I suppose I just went a little crazy for a spell. How did you find out about Marguerite and me?'

'The police in San Francisco sent us an account of you, and in it your mother's name was given as Mattson. After much too long an interval I remembered that in *Who's Who in the Theatre*, which I had been using one night to pass the time while I waited for a telephone call, Marguerite Merriam's mother was also given as a Mattson. And since I had been looking for some connection between you and Walter, it seemed that I might have found it if you and Marguerite were cousins.'

'Yes. We were more. We were both only children. Our mothers were Norwegian, but one married in Britain and one in America. And then, when I was fifteen, my mother took me to England, and I met Marguerite for the first time. She was nearly a year older than me, but she seemed younger. Even then she was brilliant. Everything she did had a—a *shining* quality. We wrote to each other every week from then on, and every year until my parents died we came to England in the summer, and I saw her.'

'How old were you when your parents died?'

'They died in a flu epidemic when I was seventeen. I sold the pharmacy but kept the photographic side, because I liked it and was good at it. But I wanted to travel. To photograph the world and everything that was beautiful in it. So I took the car and went West. I wore pants in those days just because they were comfortable and cheap, and because when you are five feet ten you don't look your best in girlish things. I hadn't thought of using them as—as camouflage until one day when I was leaning over the engine of the car a man stopped and said: "Got a match, bud?" and I gave him a light; and he looked at me and nodded and said: "Thanks, bud," and went away without a second glance. That made me think. A girl alone is always having trouble—at least in the States she is—even a girl of five feet ten. And a girl has a more difficult time getting an "in" in a racket. So I tried it out for a little. And it worked. It worked like a dream. I began to make money on the Coast. First photographing people who wanted to be movie actors, and then photographing actors themselves. But every year I came to England for a little. As me. My name actually is Leslie, but mostly they called me Lee. *She* always called me Lee.'

'So your passport is a woman's one.'

'Oh, yes. It is only in the States that I am Leslie Searle. And not all the time there.'

'And all you did before going to the Westmorland was to hop over to Paris, and lay the track of Leslie Searle in case anyone proved inquisitive.'

'Yes. I've been in England for some time. But I didn't actually think I'd need that track. I meant to do away with Leslie Searle too. To find some joint end for Walter and him. So that it would not be apparent that it was murder.'

'Whether it was murder or just, as it turned out,

leaving Whitmore in the soup, it was a pretty expensive amusement, wasn't it?'

'Expensive?'

'One very paying photographer's business, one complete gent's outfit in very expensive suitings, and assorted luggage from the best makers. Which reminds me, you didn't steal a glove of Liz Garrowby's, did you?'

'No, I stole a pair. Out of the car pocket. I hadn't thought of gloves, but I suddenly realised how convincing women's gloves are. If there is any doubt, I mean, as to your sex. They are almost as good as lipstick. You forgot my lipstick, by the way—in the little parcel. So I took that pair of Liz's. They wouldn't go on, of course, but I meant to carry them. I grabbed them in a hurry out of my collar drawer because Walter was coming along the passage calling to know if I was ready, and later I found that I had only one. Was the other one still there in the drawer?'

'It was. With the most misleading results.'

'Oh!' she said, and looked amused and human for the first time. She thought for a little and then said: 'Walter will never take Liz for granted again. That is one good thing I have done. It is poetic justice that it should have been a woman who did that. It was clever of you to guess that I was a woman just from the outside of a little parcel.'

'You do me too much honour. It never even crossed my mind that you might be a woman. I merely thought that Leslie Searle had gone away disguised as a woman. I thought they were probably your things, and that he had gone to you. But the giving up of the whole of Searle's life and belongings puzzled me. He wouldn't do that unless he had another personality to step into.

It was only then that I began to wonder whether Searle was masquerading and wasn't a man at all. It didn't seem as wild an idea as it might have, because I had so lately seen that case of arrest for theft that turned out so surprisingly. I had seen how easily it could be done. And then there was you. Staring me in the face, so to speak. A personality all ready for Searle to dissolve into. A personality who had most conveniently been painting in Scotland while Searle was fooling the intelligentsia in Orfordshire.' His glance went to the art display. 'Did you hire these for the occasion, or did you paint them?'

'Oh, I painted them. I spend my summers in Europe painting.'

'Ever been in Scotland?'

'No.'

'You must go and see it sometime. It's grand. How did you know that Suilven had that "Look-at-me!" look?'

'That is the way it looked on the postcard. Are you Scottish? Grant is a Scottish name, isn't it?'

'A renegade Scot. My grandfather belonged to Strathspey.' He looked at the serried ranks of canvas evidence and smiled. 'As fine and wholesale and convincing an alibi as ever I saw.'

'I don't know,' she said, doubtfully, considering them. 'I think to another painter they might be far more of a confession. They're so—arrogantly destructive. And angry. Aren't they. I would paint them all differently today now that I have known Liz, and—grown up, and Marguerite has died in my heart as well as in reality. It is very growing-up to find that someone you loved all your life never existed at all. Are you married, Inspector?'

'No. Why?'

'I don't know,' she said vaguely. 'I just wondered how you understood so quickly about what had happened to me over Marguerite. And I suppose one expects married people to be more sympathetic to emotional vagaries. Which is quite absurd, because they are normally far too cluttered up with their own emotional problems to have spare sympathy. It is the unattached person who—who helps. Won't you have some more coffee?'

'You make coffee even better than you paint.'

'You haven't come to arrest me, or you wouldn't be drinking my coffee.'

'Quite right. I wouldn't. I wouldn't even drink the coffee of a practical joker.'

'But you don't mind drinking with a woman who planned long and elaborately to kill someone?'

'And changed her mind. There are quite a few people I would willingly have killed in my time. Indeed, with prison no more penitential than a not very good public school, and the death sentence on the point of being abolished, I think I'll make a little list, á la Gilbert. Then when I grow a little aged I shall make a total sweep —ten or so for the price of one—and retire comfortably to be well cared-for for the rest of my life.'

'You are very kind,' she said irrelevantly. 'I haven't really committed any crime,' she said presently, 'so they can't prosecute me for anything, can they?'

'My dear Miss Searle, you have committed practically every known crime in the book. The worst and most unforgivable being to waste the time of the overworked police forces of this country.'

251

'But that isn't a crime, is it? That is what the police are there for. I don't mean: to have their time wasted, but to make sure that there has been nothing fishy about a happening. There isn't any law that can punish one for what you have called a practical joke, surely?'

'There is always "breach of the peace". It is quite wonderful what a variety of things can be induced to come under the heading of breach of the peace.'

'And what happens when you breach the peace?'

'You are treated to a little homily and fined.'

'Fined!'

'A quite inappropriate sum, more often than not.'

'Then I shan't be sent to prison?'

'Not unless you have done something that I don't yet know about. And I wouldn't put it past you, as they say in Strathspey.'

'Oh, no,' she said. 'No. You really do know all about me. I don't know how you know all you do, if it comes to that.'

'Our policemen are wonderful. Hadn't you heard?'

'You must have been pretty sure that you knew all about me before you came looking for that brown fleck in my iris.'

'Yes. Your policemen are wonderful too. They looked up the births in Jobling, Conn., for me. The infant that Mr and Mrs Durfey Searle took with them when they left Jobling for points south, was, they reported, female. After that I would have been surprised to death if there had been no brown fleck.'

'So you ganged up on me.' Her hands had stopped shaking, he noticed. He was glad that she had reached the stage of achieving a flippancy. 'Are you going to take me away with you now?'

'On the contrary. This is my farewell to you.'

'Farewell? You can't have come to take farewell of someone you don't know.'

'Where our mutual acquaintance is concerned I, as they say, have the advantage of you. I may be quite new to you—or practically new—but you have been in my hair for the last fourteen days, and I shall be very glad to get you out.'

'Then you don't take me to a police station or anything like that?'

'No. Not unless you show any signs of beating it out of the country. In which case an officer would no doubt appear at your elbow with a pressing invitation to remain.'

'Oh, I'm not going to run away. I am truly sorry for what I have done. I mean, for the trouble—and I suppose the—the misery I have caused.'

'Yes. Misery is the appropriate word, I feel.'

'I am sorry most of all for what Liz must have suffered.'

'It was gratuitously wicked of you to stage that quarrel at the Swan, wasn't it?'

'Yes. Yes, it was unforgivable. But he maddened me so. He was so smug. So unconsciously smug. Everything had always been easy for him.' She saw the comment in his face, and protested: 'Yes, even Marguerite's death! He went straight from that into Liz's arms. He never really knew desolation. Or fear. Or despair. Or any of the big, *grinding* things in life. He was quite convinced that nothing irretrievable would ever happen to him. If his "Marguerite" died there would always be a "Liz" there. I *wanted* him to suffer. To be caught in something that he couldn't get out of. To meet trouble and for once be stuck with it. And you can't say I wasn't right! He'll never be so smug again. Will he? Will he, then!'

'No, I suppose not. Indeed, I'm sure not.'

'I'm sorry Liz had to be hurt. I would go to prison if I could undo that. But I've given her a much better Walter than the one she was going to marry. She really is in love with that poor egotistical wretch of a creature, you know. Well, I've made him over for her. I'll be surprised if he isn't a new man from now on.'

'If I don't go, you'll be proving to me that you are a public benefactor instead of an offender under breach-of-the-peace.'

'What happens to me now? Do I just sit and wait?'

'A constable will no doubt serve you solemnly with a summons to appear at a magistrate's court. Have you a lawyer, by the way?'

'Yes, I have an old man in a funny little office who keeps my letters till I want them. He's called Bing, Parry, Parry, and Bing, but I don't think he is any of them, actually.'

'Then you had better go and see him and tell him what you have done.'

'All of it?'

'The relevant bits. You can probably leave out the quarrel at the Swan, and anything else that you're particularly ashamed of.' She reacted to that, he noticed. 'But don't leave out too much. Lawyers like to know; and they are almost as unshockable as the police.'

'Have I shocked you, Inspector?'

'Not noticeably. You've been a pleasant change from the armed robberies and the blackmail and the confidence tricks.'

'Shall I see you when I am charged?'

'No. A lowly sergeant will be there to give evidence, I expect.'

He took his hat and prepared to go, looking once more at the one-man show of the West Highlands.

'I really ought to take a picture with me as a souvenir,' he said.

'You can have any one you want. They are going to be obliterated anyhow. Which would you like?' It was obvious that she did not quite know whether he was serious or not.

'I don't know. I like Kishorn, but I can't remember Kishorn being as aggressive as that. And if I took the Coolin there would be no room for me in the room too.'

'But it's only thirty inches by——' she was beginning, and then understood. 'Oh. I see. Yes, it is intrusive.'

'I don't think I have time to wait and choose. I must leave it, I'm afraid. But thank you for the offer.'

'Come back one day when you have more time and choose at your leisure,' she said.

'Thank you. I may do that.'

'When the court has made an honest woman of me.' She went to the stairs with him. 'It's a bit of an anti-climax, isn't it? To set out to kill someone and end with breach of the peace.'

The detachment in this caught his attention, and he stood for a long moment looking at her. After a little he said, as one giving judgment: 'You're cured.'

'Yes, I'm cured,' she said sadly. 'I shall never be green again. It was lovely while it lasted.'

'It's nice grown-up, too,' Grant said comfortingly, and went away down the stairs. When he opened the door he looked back to find that she was still there watching him. 'By the way,' he said, 'what are accessories?'

'What? Oh!' She laughed a little. 'Belts and bibs and bows and brash little bouquets for women to put in their hair.'

'Goodbye,' Grant said.

'Goodbye, Detective-Inspector Grant. I am grateful to you.'

He went away into the sunlight, at peace with the world.

As he walked down to the bus stop a lovely mad notion came to him. He would ring up Marta and ask her if she wanted another woman for Saturday night, and she would say yes, bring anyone you would like, and he would bring them Lee Searle.

But of course he could not do that. It would be sadly unbecoming in an officer of the Criminal Investigation Department; indicating a lightness of mind, a frivolity, that could only be described as deplorable in the circumstances. It was all very well for the Lee Searles of this world, people who had not yet quite grown up, to indulge their notions, but for adults, and sober adults at that, there were the convenances.

And of course there were compensations. Life was entirely constructed of compensations.

The fantastical was for adolescents; for adults there were adult joys.

And no joy of his 'green' years had ever filled his breast with a more tingling anticipation than the thought of Superintendent Bryce's face when he made his report this morning.

It was a glorious and utterly satisfying prospect.

He could hardly wait.